WALK BACK FROM MONKEY SCHOOL

walk back from monkey school

short stories by

KATE HILL CANTRILL

Press 53
Winston-Salem

Press 53, LLC
PO Box 30314
Winston-Salem, NC 27130

First Edition

Cover image licensed through Getty Images. All rights reserved.
Cover background image licensed through Shutterstock.
All rights reserved.

Cover design by Emily Cantrill

Author photo by Serge J-F. Levy © 2012
www.sergelevy.com

This is a work of fiction. Names, characters, places, and incidents
are products of the author's imagination or are used fictionally.
Any resemblance to actual events, locales, or persons,
living or dead, is entirely coincidental.

Printed on acid-free paper
ISBN 978-1-935708-63-6

To the man who knows which way the wind blows:
John Cantrill

Oh what a happy day!

acknowledgments

The author wishes to thank the editors of the publications where the following stories from this collection first appeared.

"Guess Who Was at the Party?" appeared in *StoryQuarterly*.

"Flowing, Flown" appeared in *3rd Bed*.

"Dear England, Please Send Me a Redheaded Boy" appeared in *Blackbird*.

"This, about the Man I Met Out Here in Nearly Nowhere" appeared in *Caketrain*.

"How to Best Say Goodbye to a Very Old House" appeared in *Caffeine Destiny*.

"Oops" appeared in *Del Sol Review*.

"The Tree That Took Brooke's Faith Away" appeared in *Diagram*.

"Too Huge" and "The Hills in Pittsburgh Are So Steep They Sometimes Turn to Stairs" appeared in *Everyday Genius*.

"Come to Me at Night" appeared in *Matchbook*.

"Dead Dog Rising" appeared in *Smokelong Quarterly*.

"In the Hollow of the Hands" and "XOXO" appeared in *Pindeldyboz*.

"We Threw These At Each Other," "Two Boys in Love-ish," and "Dog Park" appeared in *Quickfiction*.

"Temporary Housing" appeared in *Salt Hill*.

"To the Woman Who Sat With Her Back to the Door" appeared in *Sleepingfish*.

"Jenny Whistled through the Mail Slot" appeared in *Swink*.

"Flutter In Night" appeared in *Vestal Review*.

"Cool Like Fire" appeared in *Wet Ink*.

"You Don't *Know* Me" and "Baking Red Delicious" appeared in *Wigleaf*.

walk back from monkey school

guess who was at the party?

She didn't look a thing like his girlfriend. This alone should have been a sign that she was just a fling, a diversion from what he had known for the past five years. She began to think of his girlfriend as Guess Who. Guess Who was at the opening, people would say. Guess Who RSVP'd yes for the party. Guess Who was wearing a half-shirt and showing her midriff. Guess Who got a dye job.

The city had never been smaller. Everywhere she went she saw him, saw her, or worse, saw them together. They looked wrong together, that was obvious to everyone, but still, when she saw them and when she would look down and pretend not to, it made her stomach wrench. Guess Who was small, terribly small, small like illness, which, she thinks is all part of the reason why he felt he should stay. Guess Who looked like she might just fall over at any minute. Sometimes she thought of flicking her—just walking up to her and flicking her shoulder with her long pointer finger and Guess Who would go toppling forward, knocking her teeth out on the sidewalk.

He was solid, too solid probably, more like thick. He had some bad points, which she tried to focus on. Grooming was an issue, although sometimes it was sweet—the little tufts of nose hairs that crept out in a laugh, the way his hair stuck up like enthusiasm—but certainly this sweetness would pass and she would be left with him, disheveled and thick. Although, after five years, Guess Who didn't seem to mind, or at least, didn't seem to think that they were points important enough to let him go over. Maybe she even liked his faults. Maybe they kept him with her. Maybe he looked in the mirror sometimes and thought, *No one else would have me.* Insecurity can make you feel safe, sometimes.

She would have him, though—faults and all. She liked how he was tall like her, not like other men who just kept shrinking. No, he was tall (it was all in his legs, but even so), and when they walked hand in hand she didn't feel at all like she was walking a dog—stopping to allow him to keep up. They had the same rhythm, and sometimes, after coffee, they both got crazy and laughed and bounced down the street and talked about things that last forever—houses, kids, friendship. That's how it started, see, with the friendship, that was how she was able to get so close without Guess Who getting territorial. She wasn't trying to mess things up, she just heard how sad he sounded whenever he'd say, *I have to go home now.*

He is still confused, however. He still calls sometimes and just says, *Hey.* It is a small city, after all, and so it happens quite often that he sees her. Mostly she is walking alone and quickly because she has things to do, many many things. She keeps herself very busy which he admires. Guess Who doesn't have a job. Guess Who used to bake but worked somewhere where termites fell from the ceiling into her cakes and so she quit. Lame, she thinks. Guess Who couldn't cut it. She bakes too. He used to love her baking because it always flopped but tasted like heaven. He told her every cake should fall apart and every pie should sink, otherwise they're just too pretty to eat. Guess Who makes beautiful cakes.

The last she heard through the network of friends involved

in the matter was that he's not with Guess Who anymore. (Not that there *is* any matter anymore for her, she dropped out. She said, Have him, and walked away—she was tired). Fantastic, she thought, just what I need. After all the back and forth and back again, now that he was forth, she wanted him to stay that way—just to keep her sane. Didn't he at least owe her that, a little bit of sane?

She was going to a party, it was one that she had every right to attend. Unfortunately, it was also one that Guess Who had every right to attend. It was a party of Mutual Friend. She got her hair cut. She bought a new shirt. She wore the shoes she sometimes felt bad for being so fancy in the back of her closet. She put sparkles on her eyelids and gloss on her lips. She had a good smile and was going to use it that night. She practiced at home telling jokes to her sister's iguana. *You guana go to? I guana have a shot of Jack before I leave.*

At the door, she rang the bell and Guess Who just happened to walk up behind her. Guess Who said *Hi*, like she meant it. Funny, she thought and grumbled something. All things considered, they shouldn't be talking. All things included the fact that she slept with Guess Who's man and she fell for him and she waited—not so patiently—for him to choose her, which he didn't. Guess Who was well aware of the facts, but was friendly as fire there at the door. Guess Who said, *He's not coming. I haven't talked to him, have you?* She just grumbled something and then ran inside the door as fast as she could. Guess Who yelled behind her, *I like your shoes!*

She immediately drank enough to feel comfortable and then alternated a drink with water so as not to lose her edge completely—she felt somewhat on the defensive lately. She noticed Guess Who drank quite a lot. She was a little afraid that Guess Who would become the life of the party and so she kept an eye on her. She tried to laugh a little bit more and a little bit louder. She laughed at a guy who looked like 'Where's Waldo' and who explained to her that he liked natural women. By this he meant hairy and so she was out of the picture. She also laughed at a man who was visiting from Cali, as he called it, and said her aura was all flipped out. *Come to Cali,* he said. *We have yard sales.*

She left him and headed for Mutual Friend when guess who appeared at her navel. Guess Who said, *Hey* and *What's up* and other odd and bothersome things. Again she grumbled and tried to talk to Mutual Friend, whose eyes grew wide like fright when she saw her standing next to Guess Who. She could never tell whom Mutual Friend sided with more, which made her a bit uneasy. She'd like to be able to talk about Guess Who when the subject came up. She would like to say something like, *I had a dream that I was carrying a beautiful old carpet bag and when I opened it Guess Who was inside and so I closed it up and sold it at a vintage store;* but she didn't. She would like to say (mostly when she saw him and Guess Who walking all out of sync holding hands) that she could eat *two* Guess Whos and still not be full, but she didn't. Instead, she tried to walk away from the situation but Guess Who followed her. She walked away quickly and sat on the floor, which was a mistake because then guess who had a better vantage point to talk to her face. *What do you want?* she finally said. Guess Who just smiled.

She is an artist and is known for putting stickers on people at parties—kind of like walking, talking public art. This time she had some that said, THIS SIDE UP, and everyone got a kick out of finding them on their pants pockets, shirt sleeves and shoe tops. One man took it off of his shirt and put it on his groin. He just wanted a reason to point there, she thought, men like that sort of thing. She was just about to begin to have a good time when she noticed Guess Who following her again. *Your hair looks good*—Guess Who said that. *I dyed mine; can you tell?* Guess Who's eyes were droopy and she looked like she'd be even easier to topple over. She thought maybe if she just blew in her general direction, Guess Who might fall over, and jam her eye in on the end of the table. This was the kind of thing she thought but didn't say out loud. She felt someone touching her back and she turned and Guess Who was there. *What are you doing?* she asked the little illness, but Guess Who just laughed. A few minutes later, Mutual Friend walked over and risked the appearance of taking sides by telling her that her back was covered in stickers that said, THIS SIDE UP. *Who did it?* she asked, although she already knew. Guess who? said Mutual Friend. Guess Who,

She went into the bathroom and took off her shirt to remove the stickers. One was flattering, meant you were a part of things; many were humiliating. She looked in the mirror and decided that she still looked good and went back into the party. Guess Who was outside the door. She was leaning on the wall and looking like she might fall over all by herself. Guess Who said, *I haven't talked to him have you?* and started to cry. She said nothing and tried to walk away but Guess Who grabbed her and pulled her down to her face. She's trying to kiss me, she thought and she pulled back fast. Guess Who fell down. Mutual Friend came over and gave her an evil look. *She tried to kiss me,* she said, and then, realizing that would never be believed said, *she tried to hit me.* Mutual Friend arranged to have Someone take Guess Who home. Someone was short and stocky and put Guess Who's arm over his shoulder and walked her out. She looked like a child—her feet weren't quite working like they should. She felt bad for her and yelled up that, no, she hadn't talked to him either. Guess Who just lifted her head and looked at her and smiled.

we threw these at each other

Jimmy wore a tie to top that torn green tee he toted every day, every other. He smelled of dirt, said he had a feeling we had watermelon somewhere since he caught a whiff from his room inside his house across the street.

That's not why I'm here, he said. I'm here to see the lady of the house.

What *lady*? I asked. You're ten years old. What lady do you mean?

Not you, he said, you're ten as well.

And so?

And so I'd like to see the lady.

Why the tie? I asked.

But Jimmy wouldn't answer; he waited for my mother to drag down the stairs, slip-slap her feet and sigh, *Hello*.

I'm selling toys for school, he said. I thought perhaps you'd be intrigued by my lovely marbles, my collection of balls. Your home has seemed so sad of late.

Then Jimmy tossed those balls inside—tiny rubber ones went hiding, while the naked, pink, slap-slapping soft bounced back and forth from wall to wall—like dancing, clapping, skipping, *fly!*

I held him, then, by his wrist. I said, Anything you want is yours—a slice of melon, a million bucks, my quivered heart, my *love*.

oops

OK, so oops. I messed that up. I made it sexual when it was sweet. Oops. I swear it was the beer. OK I lie. I always lie. I tried to be a different girl for you. So oops. I messed that up. I made it sexual when it was sweet.

I knew a woman who wrote instead 'opps' due to learning disabilities, although I thought it fucking brilliant; and when she said: My business plan? Laundromat and Coffee Shop, I nearly fainted with impression. *Opps.* And so so needed. Cleanse and energize. Just think of the aroma. Eye-watering aroma.

So when I oops-ed, when I made it sexual when it was sweet, I meant I want to be a part of you. I want to hold you in my palm. I want to cup you on my tongue. I want to suck in air and in the air—*surprise!*—it's you and you are wearing flip flops. Oops. I messed that up. I swear it was the beer. OK I lie. I always lie. I tried.

OK so you are wearing flip flops. I hold you in my palm I cup you on my tongue I breathe in air and in the air—surprise! It's you.

She didn't *say* opps; she only wrote it. And when I pointed this out she said: learning disabilities. Differences, I said. No, she said. I see one p when really there are two. And really, she said, I don't care a whole lot anyway. Oops.

But still she wrote it like that every time. Opps. Then she'd cross it out and try again. Opps. (Cross-out). Opps. (Cross-out). Opps.

I made it sexual when it was sweet. I tried.

It was brilliant. The smell of soap, the sounds of cloth rolling, rolling, and water steaming through the silver tubes, the look of milk in both the rooms: The Laundromat. The Coffee Shop. The chalk board reading: Moka lahtay. Cappah Cheeno. Mufinns. Opps.

I guess I thought that if I was a part of you—you in my palm, you anywhere—I would get there by being a different girl for you. So I made it sexual. Oops. I messed that up. I just wanted. I wanted to breathe in air and in the air surprise it's you and you are wearing those fucking goddamn flip flops.

I thought it brilliant.

If you spilled your latte when you folded who would care? Simply throw the pants into the wash. Opps. Into the wash. Into the steaming milky. Have a lahtay while it rolls.

What must you think of me? You know something of me now. Fucking brilliant. And so so needed.

I made it sexual. When it was sweet.

I tried to be a different girl. Oops. I messed that up.

But this of you I know:

I know you'll venture home at night.

At night you'll wash your feet.

And when the water touches soap you'll think: How perfect this, how very needed at this time.

XOXO

Alexandra, who at eighteen prefers to be called Zan, is no good, better yet, *lousy* at playing "Strip and Dare Quarters" (plunk!). Dana, the cousin Adam brought in from Jersey, is far superior and has yet to remove her panties—Dana is skinny and shy and so this is all for the best. Adam and Elijah are skinny, but no way are they shy; they are itching to get out of their boxers for certain. Gary is out of his and was teased that he botched a turn in order to get out of them. Gary said he wasn't prepared for *No stinking naked game* and therefore wore his awful Tighty Whities and all present asked, *Who would not botch a turn to get out of those?*

Zan has just (clink!) sent Elijah over to the keg to place his most treasured part upon the ice. She has no idea what sort of request this is.

"Just let him take his shorts off, Zan. That's just, no, no, too cruel, girl, too cruel." Gary shakes his head and shifts in his seat.

"I didn't know," Zan says. "I change my dare, Elijah. Just take your shorts off." But he will do what she asks anyway. He will count to five and squeeze his eyes shut while he lays his body down. She knows this is some sort of sweet, messed-up gesture of love he is making. Well, not *love* exactly, but whatever that is that he is feeling that made him look directly at her when Bad Company, on the tape player, sang how they *Feel Like Making Love*. Where does one look when

9

someone is facing you and mouthing those words directly at you? She looked at his left ear, which is as close as she could get to his eyes without blushing. He lights a fire in her that she is not quite used to yet. It is the kind of fire that can be nothing but bad news because Elijah's girlfriend, Zan's almost best friend Rachael, is just away for the summer and has a heart that is fragile as soufflé.

In the morning Zan goes to her baby-sitting job. *It's a good gig,* she tells her friends, because she can steal packs of mentholated cigarettes from their pantry. Secretly, she loves the boy, Raymond, whom she calls, Rummy, and sometimes, Rum-a-lum, and who is just three years old and already wears glasses. He also has a misplaced heart that sits on the outside of his little breast plate so that when he removes his protection vest, Zan can see it pumping there behind his skin—rum-a-lum, rum-a-lum. She thinks he's an extra special sort of someone.

Zan plans to return to Gary's house after Rummy's father comes home and takes his boy in his arms and blows berries on his belly. Rummy's father smells of clean sweat and she sucks in a nose-full before she leaves. Gary lives a subway stop away and because it is another hot-as-heck day, she decides to go underground. This has been the hottest summer she can ever remember—it has been over one hundred degrees with zero rain for more than five days now. Her mother's home forever toasts and this is why she avoids it so. She misses being with her brother, Frederick, though—sweet, slouching Frederick. "He got the brunt," she always says to friends who ask why he is the way he is. By this, she means he was the most hurt when their father took off to search for his lost sanity.

Once she emerges from the underworld, which was not much cooler than the street, Zan walks up Fourth to the Wiccan and Occult shop and rings the bell. Gary's mother is the owner of the shop and their house is just beyond the storeroom. As Gary walks through the store with Zan, he grabs some sandalwood incense from the counter. As he bends forward, a bead of sweat drips from under his head of curls. Zan once thought of running her hands through that mess of curls because Gary mixed up the word 'clear' with 'clairvoyant,' as in, *the glass door was so clean and clairvoyant, the bird flew right into it,* which Zan thought was very sweet; but alas, Gary is a go-nowhere sort of guy.

"The pool's filled," Gary says. "Grab a beer from the fridge and come on out."

"Mom still gone?" Zan asks.

"Wiccan convention."

"Same one?"

"No," he says, "a new one. That last one was for Occult shops. This one is just Wicca lifestyle. It's in Arizona."

Zan hears Arizona and her chest tightens, as her father's recent letters reveal that this is where he has settled, on an environmental bell-making community in the desert. She grabs a beer from the fridge and joins her friends in the tiny cement courtyard.

"Happy Thursday," Adam says.

"It's Wednesday," she says.

He shrugs. "Same diff."

They are all lounging either in or around a small, plastic baby pool. No one is wearing anything more than their underwear. *You've seen it once and you've seen it,* and so underwear and Chinese beer is what they'll do from here on out. Zan removes her excess clothing and sits where her feet can feel the cool that the rest of her body is craving. She thinks this may be heaven. She smokes a bowl and knows it for sure. She waits for Elijah to show. When he does, he will find a way to take her aside and tell her in a deep-down low voice that he has made a mix tape for her— one side is called, *Something* and the other, *Nothing At All. Namaste,* he will say, *soon we must find time alone.*

From the stereo someone will be singing about Jesus being just all right. Oh yeah.

In the early morning Zan returns home to check in. Her mother is asleep, as always, in the living room lean-back lounger, clutching a blanket to her body because the air conditioner is blowing directly on her. The look of her fingers makes Zan remember the old Polish woman who used to sweep up and down their street all day, everyday, ranting about fruit and family. Zan knows this because one day she wrote down some things that the woman said and called the Polish Community Center for some translations. *Smutney*, she remembers, sounds like smoot- nee and means sad. Zan walks past her mother and turns the AC off. She opens her eyes. Neither of them says good morning, as if they both want to avoid the fact that Zan has been out two nights and a day.

"It was cold," Zan says.

"It felt nice for awhile," Whim says. "Thank you for shutting it off."

"Would you like to move into the bedroom?"

"Too hot in there," Whim says. "Sleep now. You look weary."

Zan's bedroom looks less than lived-in these days. Recently she removed all posters and photographs to attempt a more modern look. She also painted the walls a cool, institutional green, which her mother said made her want to bash her head against them and shout obscenities. Her mother said she was sensitive to the mundane and found these walls to be holy-hell mundane. Zan has not decided yet how the walls make *her* feel, but has no problem maintaining the color so long as it troubles her mother as it does.

From her bedroom window, Zan can see that Frederick and the dog, Fiasco, are sitting in the courtyard. Fiasco, the black lab (named by Frederick when he was just three years old after hearing the word on a television commercial about an ink stain that would never come out) is dying from a large, cancerous tumor in his neck. As if the rest of his body knew it was coming, his hip has also acquired arthritis and his eyes have clouded over like a stormy day. Zan knows that Frederick loves the dog full body and soul; he was their father's dog, and she thinks this is a big part of it for her brother. Frederick spends nearly every day, all day, taking the dog for slow, pitiful walks and crushing his food with the bottom of a mason jar so that each piece doesn't seem like a stone.

Fiasco has his head in the flower patch that their mother made some time ago. Frederick is leaning against the oak tree that stands smack dab in the middle of the yard. He is wearing shorts and his thin, knotty legs are summertime dark. He is wearing a brown shirt and Zan thinks of him for a moment as another root of the tree—rough and lumped and clinging to the ground below. She walks downstairs and out the back door. Fiasco lifts his head and puts it down again. His tail whacks the cement two times—thump, thump.

"Freddy," Zan says. He wakes and smiles. "Did he mess again?"

"A little," Frederick says, "in the kitchen. He was pacing. Out here he'll just sleep and if he has to go, he'll just go." He shows her the hose he is holding to take care of Fiasco's messes.

"Come out tonight," she says. "There's a concert at the Mann and we'll all be hanging out beyond the fence."

"What concert?" he asks. "No, I can't."

"Some string quartet. It will be great."

"I have to be with Fiasco," he says. "I can't leave him."

"We'll just lie back and watch the stars. Come on, Freddy. It will be great."

"He's not well, Zan."

"He hasn't been well, Freddy."

"He's worse."

"Have you thought anymore about what we were talking

about?" Zan says. Freddy looks at her for a moment, looks at Fiasco and chokes out one sob before he holds the rest in by biting his lip. "You decide, Freddy," she says. "If you think it's time, just let me know." She kisses him on the head. He smells oily and dusty—almost the way Rummy does after playing in the park, although on Frederick the smell does not seem innocent so much as neglectful. She leans down and kisses Fiasco's nose one, two, three times. "What a fiasco, what a fiasco," she says as she pulls on his ear. His tail pounds the cement again and again. "You are the best dog ever. Every dog should be like you." She stands up and pats her brother's head. "I'm taking a nap."

He grabs a string from her cut-off shorts and yanks it as she walks away.

"Don't stay out on this cement too long," she hollers. "You'll get hemorrhoids and no girl will want to date a kid with hemorrhoids."

An argument ensues over the dessert course of lunch. Zan accuses her mother of serving her father's favorite food. Frederick tells Zan she's crazy so she screams and pounds the table. Fiasco jumps and slips while trying to stand. Whim starts crying. Frederick picks up a small watering can and throws it at Zan's head. It hits her and clink clanks onto the concrete. She grabs the back of her head with her hands.

Whim cries, "Don't hit your sister," as she takes herself and the ice cream into the house. Fiasco licks his paw.

At the concert, Zan places her head in a tuft of soft grass and counts stars. Frederick lies next to her doing the same. He tears individual strings of grass from the earth and drops them onto the back his sister's hand, which is palm side down by their hips. When Zan feels her hand is covered, she turns it over to dump the pile and Frederick builds it up again. They stay this way, listening to the strings, until Elijah walks up, when they both sit up and hold onto their knees.

Elijah is wearing a pair of cut-off shorts, Birkenstock sandals, and a white tee shirt. He sits down by Zan without looking at her. Zan can see by the way that Gary and Dana are looking at them that they suspect something. She makes a point of not talking to Elijah, and then realizes that this most likely makes things worse. She tries to speak, but nothing comes out. She feels they have left that place that would allow for small talk. Everything they share now must take them further to where they can be together for real.

Frederick lets go of his knees and lies back down. Zan does the same.

"Am I crazy, Freddy?" she asks him.

"No more than the next guy," he says.

"Was I crazy about the food?"

"I don't think you were," Frederick says, "but I don't think she did it on purpose."

"Why am I such a rotten, no-good person, Freddy?"

Freddy seems to consider this and says, "Did you know that in some cultures running amok used to mean going on a murder spree and killing everyone in sight? It was actually admissible as a defense. "Your honor," he says in a bogus voice, "I am sorry I beheaded twelve people, but sir it was not my fault as I was simply running amok." He laughs and puts something in Zan's hand. She brings it to her face and sees that it is the top of a dandelion.

"Gruesome," she says. Then she feels, more than sees, Elijah lie back and place his head next to hers on the grass. She stares hard into the sky until she feels his eyes on her. She turns to look at him.

"Zantastic," he whispers. "Open your hand."

She feels something cold placed into her palm. It is so cold she feels it burn a hole into her skin. She waits a moment and brings it to her face. It's a crystal on a rope.

"Hematite stone," he whispers. "It has something to do with love and passion."

But she knows the stone is really meant to ground one in reality. That, and ward off evil spirits when you move into a new home. These things she learned from her father. These are the sorts of things her father taught her.

"Thank you," she says, as she slips it inside her pocket. He brushes the back of her hand with his finger and electricity moves through her. She feels Frederick try to get her attention by tapping her other hand, but she continues to look at Elijah as his eyes— the deepest brown she has ever seen—are saying things she's only dreamt of. This, Zan thinks, is *for real*. Out of the corner of her eye she sees Frederick stand up and slump off. From the stage beyond the fence comes the high pitched cry of a lone violin. She is, she is sure of it, in another, more wonderful world.

When they return home that night, later than they told Whim they would be, Frederick, after checking on Fiasco, takes Zan to his room to show her the latest postcard that came that day from their father. This one is a picture of the bell-making environmental community where he is currently living. It looks to Zan like someone made a mistake with stone in the middle of the desert. The sand can almost pass for snow it is so white.

"Dearest Alexandra and Frederick," she reads aloud. "Did you know that some ancient peoples ate soil and clay to survive? What a treasure this world is! XOXO Much love, Dad." She looks at her brother. "*Peoples?*" she says. "Our father is bizarre, Freddy."

"Don't say that," he says.

"*Acting* bizarre," she corrects.

"Don't say that," he repeats and then, squinting his eyes, asks, "If you *had* to eat dirt, what dirt would you eat?"

"Mom's flower patch," she says.

"Mom's flower patch," Frederick agrees. "No question."

On Monday Zan cares for Rummy. Over the weekend she made plans for Elijah to come over during Rummy's nap, but now, with the sweet little boy swaying back and forth in her arms, she thinks better of it. She holds her arms around him tightly, but without putting pressure on his vulnerable body—more like a cage than an embrace. She kisses his head. He adjusts the strap on his glasses and spins his whole body around to look at her. His quick movements make her nervous; she is always aware of his heart, although she knows that he is more aware of it than anyone. He knows which movements feel right and which do not. He has his vest on too, so, according to his doctor, he is just like any other three-year-old boy. This, Zan can never believe.

"Will you be here tomorrow, Zan?" Rummy asks.

"Yes," she says, "I'll be here tomorrow."

"Will you be here the day after that?" he asks.

"Yes, and the day after that."

"And the next day, too?"

"Yes, Rummy, and the next day, too."

"You want to live here? I'm not using my crib anymore."

"No, Rummy. I have my own family to live with."

"Maybe just for awhile?" he asks.

"No," she says, "Not for awhile. I need to be with my own family. My brother and my mother and my dog."

"You have babies?"

"You know I don't have any babies, Rum-a-lum. You ask me that all the time."

"Aunt Theresa has a baby. It came out of here." He takes his open palm and brushes it slowly over Zan's breasts. She laughs and moves his hand to her stomach. He laughs and puts it back on her breasts. They play like this for a bit, until the boy decides that he has grown tired and he places his head, glasses and all, on her chest. She suddenly feels too thin. She leans back in the sofa so his head moves down into the softer parts of her. In this way they sleep.

Zan goes home instead of to Gary's after babysitting. She took Rummy to the park during his normal naptime and fears that Elijah showed up at the house as they had planned. She was afraid that once she saw him, she would let him inside, but she just couldn't do that. That little boy with his exposed heart deserves better and around Elijah, she feels she is a very small person. She will deal with this over the phone instead of at Gary's. Her gut feels pinched over it, nonetheless. How real is this to him, anyhow? Does he think of her as she thinks of him? Does he think of her as someone who he will think of even after they have both moved away for school? Does he think of her like she is worth losing Rachael over? Does she think that *he* is? She wonders why there is no handbook for things like this. There should be rules that people follow when it comes to love. Love should be reliable and should never, ever just drift away.

When she enters her home, Frederick stands at the bottom of the stairs. For a shiver of a moment, she thinks he is her father. Frederick looks gaunt and unhappy and this makes him remind her of her father.

"Are you lost, too?" she asks him.

"It's time, Zan," he says.

She follows him into the kitchen where Fiasco lies wrapped in a blanket, breathing erratically. Whim sits by him, her face swollen from tears. Zan feels angry and would like to hit someone. For the first time in awhile, instead of wanting to hit her mother, she would like to hit her father. She pictures herself reaching from here to Arizona and whacking his head into a bell mold he has just dug. His head rings like something hollow. Her anger quickly dissipates into grief and she kneels down to kiss the dog.

"What a fiasco," she cries. His eyes do not see her. She straightens up and wipes her face. "I'll drive," she says. "Mom?"

"Yes, you drive," Whim says.

Frederick bends down and gathers up the almost lifeless shell of a dog and lifts him without effort. Zan and her mother clear the way and open doors. The veterinary clinic is just a few blocks away and Zan finds parking almost right in front of it.

Inside, the vet is waiting for them. He tells them to place the dog on the table and he gives them a few minutes alone with him. Zan thinks she might lose it and fears for her brother. She is surprised, then, when the vet administers the shot and Frederick pets the dog's head calmly until he stops breathing, and then stands tall as if relieved when the breathing stops. It is Frederick who puts the blanket over Fiasco's lifeless body and it is Frederick who speaks cool and collected to the vet about the ashes. Will they be mixed with the ashes of other dogs? Can he guarantee that they won't? It is Frederick who chooses a simple box for the ashes to be contained in and who says, "I'll write to Dad," as he leads Zan and Whim, both crying, out the door.

Zan hands the car keys to her mother and says, "You drive," and she turns and walks down the street and into the subway station. The urine smell sickens her more than usual and she feels like she could vomit. She waits for the subway and listens to the high pitched cries of far-away cars. Hot breezes blow through the tunnels, like gaseous waves leftover from a long-gone train. She will forever feel trapped when in this underground world.

When she gets to Gary's, instead of going in the front door, she walks around to the alley and tip toes over weeds, broken glass and garbage until she gets to the back of Gary's courtyard. She stands on a loose brick and stretches over the wall to see who is in the yard. It is starting to get dark, but she can clearly see Gary is packing a bowl, his feet in the plastic pool. There is no sign of Elijah. She steps down off the brick and walks back out into the street. As she emerges from the alley, she barely misses bumping into Elijah, who is heading towards Gary's. He grabs her by her shoulders.

"Zantastic? What are you doing in the alley?"

She begins to make up a story, but then stops. She takes

his face in her hands and pulls him to her. She kisses him and for a second, he kisses her back. His mouth is cool and tastes like cherry water ice. He stops kissing her and pushes her away.

"Whoa," he says right before he grabs her and pulls her back into the alley, where they kiss again. He moves his hands feverishly over her body, without the intense coolness he usually exhibits. She finds this both exciting and disappointing at the same time; now there is the question of who is in control. She bangs her head on the concrete wall. She fills with liquid electricity from her throat to her thighs. He bangs his teeth into her teeth. She grabs his knitted rainbow belt and pulls him as close as she can. He steps on the edge of her sandal, so when she moves her foot, the sandal stays and her foot is bare. She lifts her leg and wraps it around his waist. He lifts her and then drops her as he fumbles with his belt. She stumbles as she lands on garbage and a piece of broken wood scrapes her ankle.

"Dammit," Elijah says. "Come on."

He grabs her hand and she barely has time to slip her foot into her sandal before he takes her down the alleyway, across a street, behind a church and through an iron fence that leaves just enough space for their heads to pass through where it meets up with a hot brick wall.

He pulls her through the graveyard until he gets to a headstone that is tall enough to hide behind. She feels eyes upon her as he lifts her shirt and bra; even so, she unhooks his button-fly and slips one leg out of her own cut-offs and panties. Her head is pressed hard into the tall stone slab as Elijah's weight bears down on her and she digs her nails into the dirt. There are voices all around them. The streets and sidewalks are filled with cars and people walking and she suspects that they are barely hidden in the shadows. Elijah kisses her neck and she turns her head and she smells dry earth and thirsty grass and rotting garbage from a trash can somewhere. She feels herself being pressed into the soil deeper and deeper as Elijah moves into her. She shuts her eyes and imagines falling through a cool black hole of earth. She is floating, as if pumped with air and pushed into the hollow space in the center of the world. There is no light, only air and heat left from things long gone.

Elijah shudders and collapses into her arms. She places her face into his neck where his skin is hot, and his sweat is cool. She is happy to feel his weight, his heart, and to taste his saltiness. She takes his earlobe into her mouth and keeps it there until he pulls away.

"There's blood," he whispers.

She slides back into her cut-offs, sits up and looks at her ankle. "Something cut me in the alley." Elijah sits back on his feet with his hands propped on his knees and squints at her, questioning. She looks around and sees that they are very much in the public eye. He laughs a little when he realizes and says, "We better blow this joint, kid."

They blow through the fence and behind the church and part ways on the street, even though Elijah thinks they can totally make something up, man, so Gary will have no reason to suspect anything, but Zan decides she'd like go home and be with her family, to recall something—she's not certain what—but something sweet and vital.

At home there is a message for her from Rachael, who says *Hey Zany, give me a call.* She doesn't call her, but instead puts on her most comfortable clothes and watches the television with her mother and brother. She accepts when Whim offers her some ice cream. The house feels very different to Zan now. It feels like the walls are right there next to her body, but not because the rooms got smaller, but because Zan feels so much larger. Her body feels as big and light as a hot air balloon; she is being lifted by warm air flowing up inside the world within her. She thanks her mother for the ice cream, but really she is thanking her for the house, because without it, she fears that she would completely fill with air and float away and be lost forever.

Zan convinces Frederick to come baby-sit with her the following day—Rummy's parents have been looking for someone to take over for Zan when she moves, and she thinks that Frederick just might be a good choice. Rummy's parents are particularly cautious about who they will leave their boy with and would require him to meet with the doctor to learn some specific emergency procedures, like how to perform CPR on a child lacking a ribcage. They walk a few blocks to the park and find that, despite the heat, it is mottled with kids flailing around and she is glad to have Frederick's help in watching the boy's heart.

Rummy and Frederick adore each other and for a moment, Zan feels a tinge of jealousy over the affection that the child shows to her brother. She understands, though, because Frederick has a sweetness about him that certain special people can see. He is tall, too, and when he lifts the boy over his head, Rummy is higher than the all the other kids in the park—free from being hurt by anything they throw or kick. With Frederick there, Zan can sit back and watch from afar, while her brother protects the boy's heart with his body.

She finds a bench and sits. Although she trusts Frederick, she continues to predict the next moves of the more spastic children running around. There is a particularly rambunctious boy who insists on tossing stones who she is slightly wary of. She is about to point him out to Frederick, when she hears her name.

"Hey, Zantastic."

She turns and sees Elijah. He stands behind the bench in a pose that makes it look like he's been there for awhile—as if his feet have settled into the earth below. The sun is directly above him and she must squint to look at him. She stands and walks over. She wipes her brow with the back of her hand. He reaches out and flicks at her belt loop.

"How did you find me?" she asks.

"When you weren't at the house, I figured you might be here. I'm on my way to Gary's." He jams his hands in his pockets and pulls his shoulders up to his ears. He holds it a bit longer than a shrug and when he relaxes he exhales with such vehemence that Zan can smell cigarette on his breath. He cocks his head to the side.

"Did Rachael call you?" he asks finally.

"No," she says. "I mean, yes, but I didn't talk to her." Zan feels her face turn red at the mention of Rachael's name, especially having it mentioned by Elijah. She wishes for a moment that she can take back everything—every rush and burn and zap of electricity that she shared with him. Now that Rachael's name is out there between them, she wants to go back to before, when things were easy and by the book. But when Elijah says that Rachael is coming home from vacation early—that her family thinks she should spend some time at home before she moves away to school—Zan is not quite sure what he means. When he scrunches his shoulders again, though, and kicks the dirt and says, "I suppose it's for the best," she thinks she may understand. And when he leans in and gives her a cool, dead-battery embrace and walks off like someone who is sorry for something, she knows for certain, that she is no longer part of his picture.

She watches him walk off until he goes around the corner. She feels drained and more numb than sad. She turns back to the playground and watches the children play. For a moment they seem like summertime insects—buzzing about with no direction or purpose but to live and to cover as much of their world as they possibly can every day that they're on it. That's the way to be, she thinks, light and airy and free to fly. She snaps out of it and searches for Frederick and Rummy. She looks on the swings and on the monkey bars. She is about to call for them when she sees them in the sandbox. Her breath stops and she freezes when she realizes that Rummy has

4 x

unbuckled the bottom of his safety vest and has it pulled up over his face—exposing his heart for Frederick. Frederick is leaning in towards the boy with his hands held open and his fingers spread wide on either side of Rummy's body. Zan sees the kid who was tossing stones and another running with a stick and another flying down the slide with hard-soled shoes and she runs towards the sandbox. Everything is a blur around her and she thinks she can almost hear that quivering heart beating—rum-a-lum, rum-a-lum, rum-a-lum. Kids run in front of her and she has to stop and start and run careful of her footing. Finally, she reaches the box and falls on her knees into the sand. By this time, however, Frederick has replaced the vest and is securing the belt on the boy's back. Rummy looks at Zan and smiles.

cool like fire

The television sparked into electric spits of light when Tommy Tyler tried to fix it. I shivered.

I can do it, he said. I only need a thingy-thingy.

I rolled my eyes and suggested he leave it alone. Leave *me* alone, too, I said, as kindly as such a thing can be said.

Tommy huffed and said, OK, Lovely. I have to make that hoisty tree-thing anyhow.

Tommy always called me *Lovely*. He called me *Glow* and *Glisten*. He said he didn't need my heart, per se; he only needed my pinky finger hooked with his and he'd be happy.

Ecstatic, he said. Zapped with bliss.

But Tommy was a go-nowhere—it was apparent in his smell, his shuffly walk and slouch—in the fact that his great aspiration was to hoist himself into a tree. Nice eyes, I thought, however.

I told my mother of the television.

Like this, I said, and spat onto the floor.

She shrugged and flicked the radio. Some one-hit wonder eked out tinny. Remember these guys? she said, and bobbed her head like dancing.

No, I said. We need a new TV.

She rubbed her fingers with her thumb. No franks, she

25

said, and then, That's French for out of luck. She lit a cig. I stomped the sparks I swore I saw fall to the floor.

Be careful, I said. It's cold in here.

She told me to put on a sweater. Wait for Spring. Father would have lit a fire, given the sparks a proper home.

You're disaster, I said. You're emergency.

You're pain, she said. You're permanent child. And then she sang the song's refrain: *Dancing in the heat of night, yeah yeah.*

Tommy *oofed* and banged against the tree.

No worries, Glow! he shouted from outside although I paid him no attention.

I sat and stared at the thick, black glass; I held the lonely plug inside my fist. I'm missing my shows, I thought. There goes the world, tick tock it's gone.

How now will I escape? I asked the cat.

Get a life, it said, and then it took a nap.

This house, I thought. This being young. This all must end someday. My reflection in the TV glass showed curves but due only to the convexity of the screen.

I went to my room and lifted the window, leaned my elbows on the sill. My metal fire ladder banged against the siding and Tommy turned and looked. He tipped a hat he didn't wear. He stepped upon a flat of wood, said, Watch this!—and tugged upon a rope. He lifted up two feet before it came apart and he fell.

You think it's really broken, Tommy?

He rubbed his head and shrugged. He walked over to my ladder, reached up and touched a rung. I looked away and so he climbed.

Your sweatshirt's filthy, I said. I can smell it from up here.

It's hole-y too, he said. He reached the top and hung there, staring.

I felt flamey-things burn around me, smelled smoke or

something like it. I pointed to his sweatshirt and found my finger slipped inside a hole and touched the skin of Tommy's tummy. You're hot, I said. You're like the summer. You've come to save me from the fire.

Then I'm saving you from yourself, he said, for you are electric bits of burning light inside of these, my cool, blue eyes.

walk back from monkey school

And hold the clammy hand of Jimmy, and kick the leaves so that their musk floats up and sneezes you, and move too fast so that your Mom-mom frets, your Mom-mom pleads, "Slow down, you two!" And think of how she'll say it later: "Their vigor turns me *sixes and sevens*"; and wonder if the term refers to your young age, and recall that you were only two when back you slammed into her teeth, slammed through her lip with just the bulbous baldness of your head, and how she cried and ran away, and how she returned each Autumn day, to walk with you and the neighbor boy after school—the school she named for monkeys.

Kick fast again into those leaves, with Jimmy who you know you love, because he smells so thick with play, because he stands as tall as you, because your Mom-mom sees those tiny devils in his smile. Let Mom-mom shuffle up behind you, her spine all twisted as a phone cord, her lovely fingers aching forward, her watered eyes paining, *Please,* into your head.

And when Jimmy moves away that day, sit on the high back of the sofa, hold your hand out for his Skittles, say nothing more than "See you later." But when Mom-mom goes that final time, so small she sits inside your own cupped palm, just push her up into the sky, and blow behind her, sending leaves and bits of air along. And miss them both: the air, the leaving.

jenny whistled through the mail slot

We all thought, *Birds!* We all thought, *Nests inside the chimney!* We crumpled to the hearth, turned wide eyes up toward the flue. Our house's mouth like morning breath, thickly caked with yesterday. Our eyes climbed up the smoker's throat. *WheetTweet. WheetTweet.*

I thought of birds swoop-swooping down. I thought of wings still damp with birth.

If they drop, our mother said, don't place your hands upon them.

But why? we asked.

Their mothers might just leave the nest, fly out above and flitter off.

I cupped my hands behind my back. I told my sisters to do the same.

Old wives tale, our father said, his hands held out before him.

Silence sunk. A chill breathed in from out.

WheetTweet.

If only we knew that chill came from the opened mail slot, the neighbor Jenny blowing through it, we might not have cared which one was right. Instead we held one hand before us, one hand back, our eyes pulled from the nest, soared back and forth between them.

When father said, I'll get the birds, and when he placed his hands upon our backs—if only we knew there were no

birds, if only we knew it was someone *out* just breezing *in*—
we might not have flown so easy with him, while mother
stayed, while mother knelt upon the stony hearth, fisting
fingers into knots.

baking red delicious

Stefan woke. He had to bake something. It was that sort of day, the way the sun poked through the storm of clouds, jester-like, waving beams by his hot face—boasting *power, control*, the gift that is *light*. Stefan saw apples, the type that sell cheap in rickety crates. He is an old man and in that truth he understands the sun and his immodest glow. *I peel apples!* Stefan said, as he dove his fist through the column of dust set afire by the light shone into his kitchen. He sat at the table and peeled the waxed red away from the meat— the true heart of the fruit.

He sat for so many hours the sun tired and withdrew his old beams. Stefan laughed. *I have the core of a young man! I have enough naked fruit to bake pies for a lifetime!* He sliced a lemon, held half in his great gnarled hand and squashed citrus over the bushel to keep it from browning—to sustain the short life of the knurled, pulpy bodies in the bowl on his table—until the crust was prepared to take them to the next world, the world that is lovely, the one of sweet pies.

in the hollow of the hands

The man who eats pigeons lives just across the street. Spit can make it from my house to his; spit can shoot from my bedroom window and land on his stoop where the cats come to feed on the less-desirable parts of the cooing, fluttering, clumsy fowl that look out forever from his basement window.

The way this street works, the nasty albino boy can whisper, *Gothic pussy*, three floors below my window and it will creep up the brick and into my room.

Mother yells from inside, "Go get me some milk! God damn it, will you do me that one, small favor?"

No I will not. Not now and not ever. She, after all, chose this.

"Damn it, how did I ever bear such a miserable piece-of-shit k¹

¹ lives way out of place—at least one block too far south—but he is big and not-friendly and he knows the way to hold a gun without looking like a poser. He stands in his doorway and makes the whole street aware. He hacks up phlegm and scratches whatever it is that he feels needs scratching. Even that pink kid with the bone-white lashes quits whispering *nigger* when 14K stands there scratching.

Scritch scratch, where's my cigarettes?

* * *

Each time I venture out I'm caught by something, it seems.

"You black on the inside, too, Gothic? Is that my dog's collar or did you get your own?"

It's mine and everyone wears black these days and you'd know it if you were still going to school. *Black celebration*— my Walkman long busted, but I continue to wear it and hold the song in my head. Stupid white-out freak. Why you always look so god damned stunned?

"What was that, pussy? My sweet Gothic girl."

"Get off our stoop."

"Can't you be a friendly kitty?"

"Move your butt off my stoop and let me inside."

"Got to get to your coffin before the sun shines too bright?"

Fucker, fuck fuck, stupid raw-meat fucker fuck.

Tony has to wear a school uniform and his dyed black hair and shiny black tie match so hotly I said he could come over even though it is against the rules. White-on-white is nowhere to be found, and I'm pissed, because Tony's dad has some interesting connections in South Philly. I forget about it quick, though. *Lips like sugar,* revenge is nothing next to something.

Whispered talk about *Spics* crawls up the brick façade. Tony looms over me, hot like a fever. When things get so good they almost hurt I want to snarl and say it, too: *spics, dego wop bitch.* Up the brick, up and up, like the albino is right there in my ear as Tony pushes deeper and deeper. *Gothic pussy. Bird-eating Polack. Nigger gangster. Gothic cunt-mother.*

A scream in life is nothing like the movies. It sounds more like play. *Fucking Hallohan High sluts goofing off.*

"Say it again," Tony says.

"Fucking Hallohan sluts!"

"Yell it! Say it louder!"

"Fucking sluts!"

Pop! Pop! They are always hanging on the corner screaming about everything, smashing bottles, tormenting boys. The Great Whiteness waits for the wind to blow their skirts up.

Tony leaves and I try to watch him from my window. Where are the girls? I listen for the albino whispers. I hear only sirens. *Woop woop.* Flashing lights. *Coo coo.* The pigeon man's door cracks open. He reaches his arm out, hooks the cat dish in his ugly fingers and pulls it inside. I can only see across the street. I press my face into the glass, turn it to the side and reach with my eyes. I hesitate before opening the window. *Enjoy the silence.* I lift it open.

14K is cradling something broken. There is blood on the black street that looks like a syrup. Further down the block a man's body is basting in the heat and looks nearly forgotten. 14K stands, empties his arms. Cops guide him away from what he protected, their hands cupped near the small of his back. I see what he held. She clutches the end of a torn purse strap. Milk spills from a carton tucked half inside the brown bag beside her. She clenches her eyes as help carries her to a gurney. *Snap* and it stands on four metal wheels.

Pss, pss, Kitty Cat. From our stoop below it creeps. *Pss, pss, don't be scared, Little Kitty. Little Cat.*

two boys in love-ish

When he said his heart felt achy, what he really meant was that his diaphragm, pulled taut, could tear like corneas; and all he ever wanted was to place his thumb into that quivered dip between the other boy's two clavicles—*click clack* bird bones sucked dry and drumming on a thin-skinned barrel—maybe then, he thought, his thumb pulsed there, he'd know what one should do when *One* wants desperately for *Two,* when one wants fingers on the softer bits: the temples, navel, backs of knees, the foot arch, earlobes, spitted cheeks, the nipples right before they *ping,* eyebrows, salt-necks, everything; but when he tried to thumb him there (his eyes held down, his face held loose to hold a hit) the other boy just turned away: Don't touch me there; it tickles, makes me feel you'll tear right through my skin and gesture to my itty monsters dancing mean upon my breastbone—*tap, boom,* hear them?—they are my gutless caverns, echo dancing. I can't possibly allow them out. Not possibly, alas, alas. Not probably. Perhaps, perhaps.

temporary housing

So I found out I had a mouse in my slummy apartment and I didn't know what the heck to do. My sister is vegetarian and anti-glue-trap like I am and she gave me this little condo trap. Actually, the manufacturers don't call it a trap; they call it a 'temporary housing situation,' which cracks me up. Anyhow, she brought it over about a week ago—it was the night I went into the hospital, which I remember clearly because we had a fight. I had a lot of dishes in the sink and they stank and she can't let things slide sometimes and she sort of flipped out on me about it and also about the fact that I can't seem to get myself together enough to call my landlord and get keys for those padlocks on the window bars and she left my place chanting, *firetrap, firetrap, firetrap,* with her face all red and wrinkled and I thought that was totally insane. I know that it came out of that whacked-out combo of love and fear that sometimes takes over people, but that was crazy, like, psycho crazy.

Anyway, she didn't have a chance to explain this temporary mouse housing to me before she went ballistic and I'm still not quite sure how to use it. I suppose I could have called her, but I don't feel like talking to her yet. I haven't felt like talking to anyone but my mother these days. Do you ever get like that? Like, get to thinking that if you pick up the phone that rock bottom is simply going to shoot up and meet your feet instead of waiting for you to get there? I don't know; I just haven't felt like talking to her, not for any particular reason, except I guess I don't want her to think that I was just being all "Drama Queen" that night or anything. I don't think she'd say that, at least not right away, but it would come out eventually. You know how things go with family.

So I'm looking at this thing and from what I can gather, I coax the mouse in with food, like a piece of cheese in the far end of the condo, and then this little switch gets tripped and a cracker that I have put inside the trap door swings down and 'temporarily houses' the mouse with a piece of cheese and a cracker that he can partially eat and decide to stay, or completely eat and decide to go?? That's where I'm not clear. That seems like a royally good deal, if you ask me, to be allowed to hang out in your very own brand spanking new condo with cheese and crackers and not have to work or worry about life outside and all. Give me some weed or cheap wine and I'd say that sounds a bit like heaven. Maybe that's my problem—maybe I have low expectations of life.

It really isn't an effective way to get a person like me to motivate, you know? Chanting *firetrap* like she's conducting some goddamn séance really does nothing but freak me the hell out and make me feel like even more of a capital L loser. It was just a super low day and my sister's timing was colossally bad. I will get to it. I will get to *everything* at some point. It's just that it takes a whole hell of a lot of energy to deal with a mouse, especially if you have the tendency, as I do, to think that animals, critters and all, have a hell of a greater right to be here (here, meaning planet earth) than we monster people with our monster cars and our monster homes and our no-good nasty trash and waste and all. You don't see mice going around depleting the ozone with their gluttonous sense of superiority. Sometimes, honestly I just think, What's the point? We are just screwing everything up more and more every year and everything is just such an astronomical mess that I can't hardly take it sometimes. I care about people; I do, but they are just so quick to *screw things up* and my sister asks me why I smoke so much and why, when I do venture out, I have to get spit-up drunk. Because it's all too much, that's why! And I am such a goddamn hypocritical part of all of it because I have a mouse in my place and I'm like, *Oh, this is my place and you must go and find another place to call home.*

Anyway, I think I'm supposed to get the mouse inside the condo and take her to a park or something and let her free. I just hope she doesn't have any family or anything because how do we know how they will feel about being separated? It could rip their hearts right out of their little chests. It could send them plummeting toward the depths of gloom. They could feel really, very lonely, like, passionate lonely. We really know nothing here on this planet and I think, at least on good days I hope, that we are getting closer to admitting that.

I'd ask my neighbors if they have mice and what they are going to do about them, but sometimes, I'm afraid of what they think of me. I know the doors to each apartment are thin and the most innocent of sounds can easily penetrate them. I'm sure they heard my sister chanting and I *know*, without a doubt, that they have heard my ex and I battling it out. My mother would have disapproved of him, had she made his acquaintance. But she didn't make it.

There's one neighbor that I kind of sometimes talk to, but I don't even know her name, which is the *worst.* I mean, she told me her name, probably repeated it once or twice too, but I can't seem to remember it. She just has an 'A' for her first name on her mailbox—I already thought of that. I think it is something kind of complicated; she looks sort of exotic with that olive-like skin I've always wanted. That stinks, though, to have to see her in the hall, or on one of those rare occasions when I muster the energy to do laundry and have to say, *Hey, neighbor!* That is *so* corny and I hate being corny. A while back she knocked on my door and I was actually standing just behind it, by my sink, smoking a bowl. I was about to shove a towel under the door when she went and knocked. I just stood still and held my breath and closed my eyes until she went away. Even when she did leave, I stood there for about a half an hour longer because she lives across the hall and can hear the floor creak. It makes me feel like someone is always watching me. It's not like I always smoke. It just helps me relax on low-down days. I've never been a really *grand* sleeper.

I just want to be clear that no, I didn't take those few extra pills because my sister went Joan Crawford on me that day. I don't want that to be a weight on her—although I'm not so sure she would put two and two together anyhow, but still, to be safe, let it be known that I just wanted to sleep, you know? My body was so tired. I have never felt so absolutely, infinitely tired in all of my twenty-two years. My feet felt cold like dead fish and my back felt like it had been hoisting furniture all day. I remember clearly that my head felt like someone else's head—like someone with a much larger head than mine had switched with me and it just sat there, all confused and too heavy for my neck. My eyes were wild, though. They were so awake and alert—looking for mice in the dark, seeing shadows on the street skulking around at god knows what hour, planning out things like grocery lists, job possibilities and life in general. I was going batty and all I really wanted to do was sleep heavy. I wanted to sleep and dream about things that have to do with water, because usually those dreams make me happy in the morning. I wanted to have dreams like I do sometimes where I am an autumn leaf flit-floating on the cool surface of a river and swishing in and out of tiny ripples and tides. That's a rare sleep and that was what I needed that night, a rare sleep.

The doctor, the mean, You-are-healthy-in-the-body-so-why-are-you-being-so-careless-with-it-by-taking-too-many-anti-depressants-you-stupid-loser, doctor in the emergency room said the number was what bugged him the most. "Bugged," that's what he said. He said if I had taken four, yeah, I was looking for sleep; five, even; but nine, no no no, that was not regular sleep in his eyes. I said, No, not regular sleep, a *rare* sleep. I just kept thinking of my two kitties and how they were going to get hungry if I wasn't home in the morning and also I was thinking that charcoal is just about the worst taste in all the world wide and I kept getting reminded of that because I puked the first cup up all over my hospital gown and it just stared at me all night. I told the nurse that I couldn't drink it and she said that the doctor would have no problem jamming a tube into my throat and pouring it down if that was what I wanted. They were all making it into such a big deal! They put an IV in me and everything! When I got up to go to the bathroom I had to drag my pole around. It was all very dramatic. I just kept thinking of my kitties and wondering if they would eventually eat the mouse if they got hungry enough. Really, I didn't even want to test that because I had no interest in getting locked up in some crazy ward with bright, fluorescent lights where they would make me take more drugs and I'd have to wear a nightgown all of the time. I saw *One Flew Over The Cuckoo's Nest* and so I know what those places are about.

Thank god my mother was with me. I was SO SMART to call to her from home when my heart started flipping out and I started sweating and my head went all manic-like on me. By the way—this is what happens when one takes too many anti-depressants—they rev you up; they don't calm you down so don't even think that or feel like you need to try it for yourself to see because it is NOT a fun feeling and you can totally die. He kept saying (the doctor), Did you know? Did you know that your kidneys or your liver would have failed you if you didn't come here? Did you know that? I said I didn't, and I guess I didn't, but you know, when you feel that much of a need for a rare sleep, information like that gets neatly shoved in the back pocket of your brain. He didn't like my creative use of words at all and said that I would have to talk with the psychiatrist to see if I knew that and so I had to wait and man, was waiting HELL! Thank god my mother was there. She wasn't always there before, you know, in the mother sense, but that night she sort of surrounded me and handled me very well. She just floated around really gently and told me what they would want to hear in order for them to allow me to leave. She suggested that I go back to my therapist—The Man With Long Pants, I call him—who I stopped seeing due to a general excess of ignorance and youth on my part. He is brilliant and really spiritual and that is more the track I am ready to take these days. (I shouldn't just say it, but I suppose it's o.k. to mention that my mother had once been in a very similar position herself—this position of a general excess of ignorance and youth, though she chose a different path). Those pills I was taking had a hold on me that just felt wrong. Don't judge it, though, the fact that I have stopped taking my "Happy Pills" unless you can say that you have been inside my exact shoes. If you did, then you'd know what a drag it is to see you, haha.

I had to try to calm down before the psychiatrist came or she'd lock me up pronto. I was very nervous—hopped up, I guess you can say, from all the pills in my system and it was a hard road coming down. My mother was great. She was once a nurse and I could feel that she was in her element there, within all the chaos of the hospital. I was really a wreck and what made it all worse was that there was a woman in the bed next to me, separated by a curtain, who was screaming because of an infection in her privates. I hate to say it, I mean I HATE to say it, but the room smelled of sick privates and I had a hell of a time not coming off as crazy in that situation. I was like, Mom, can you smell that? But she just smiled. I just kept thinking of my kitties and of the mouse and how I really didn't want them to eat her because, first of all, she is very small and wouldn't fill them up, and also, because she has lived with us for so long that it just wouldn't seem right. It would be like incest, no, wait, that's sex and I mean eating one's own— cannibalism, that's right. Anyway, I just wanted out and my body just wouldn't stop writhing and jerking and again, I'll say it again: Thank god my mother was there.

I felt her do this awesome thing that she used to do with the terminal kids whenever they were receiving shots or something painful like that, or even when they were dying— she sort of tapped on me with her light fingers in specific spots, over and over. It sounds dumb, I know, but she just tap tap tapped me on my leg when it jumped around or my arm when it twitched and it was just like she was feeding me with something through her finger. It was like she had a goddamn tube for a digit and was pouring warm milk right into the parts of me that weren't doing so hot. It was like she took care of my body for a while, so I could take some time off and just hang out without it—I could just lean my brain back against the pillows and let my blood pump through it like a stream, and I did, I *really* did, dream of water and of being a leaf flit-floating above a cool river. If anyone asks me, I am going to say that's how it was when we were curled in the womb—that a tiny, amazing tube connected straight into our middles gave us everything we needed so that we could sleep and dream and save our strength for the outside, because that was where we'd need it.

When she finally got there, clip boarded and cranky, the psychiatrist made it obvious to me that she hated me. She asked if there was anyone she should call. I looked at my mother and said no; then I went on about the room being too small for all my many fans. The psychiatrist didn't care for any of my jokes and when I asked her if she ever tasted charcoal she looked at me slit-eyed and when I said that I recommended the grape juice over the charcoal she wrote something down that I couldn't see. I had to stop myself from saying out loud that I just wanted my mother to come home with me to my place, which is not so bad because it is mine and it does keep me warm; and I really just wanted her to come inside and maybe look at my dishes and not *do* them, but maybe not mention them, either. Maybe she might see the mouse and just laugh it off, because I know she knows what it's like to not be able to hear something at a particular moment. I remember quite a few times growing up when she was not prepared to hear something—when she would just stay in bed and cover her ears with that white blanket I loved for hours and hours. I still have that blanket. I look loads like her these days. She's better off now, I suppose, sleeps soundly, but still, she understands. On the way back from the hospital, I heard her say that most people *assume* life, but a few need to *choose* it. Sometimes when she talks like this as I drive, the car slows down and I can hardly hear the motor anymore.

"Foolish" was my diagnosis. Hell, I could have told them that if only they'd have asked. I couldn't believe "foolish" was a proper diagnosis. I was thinking maybe, "complicated," or "sensitive," or "clairvoyant," even; but she gave me "foolish," probably from all the jokes and because of the charcoal puke stain down the front of my gown. Lord, I am a mess.

My place is not *terrible*. I mean, it's not the greatest apartment, but there are worse to be found. It's just that it has seen some better days and big deal if I have a mouse! I figure if there is a fire, I will be able to go out my front door. I suppose that would mean that the fire was started by me. I do like the soothing flicker of a candle once in awhile. I am militant, though, with my curling iron and I don't even own a toaster oven—there's no room on the counter for one. I'm trying to clean the place up and have gotten rid of some old things so that my space can be comforting as opposed to claustrophobic. It will be easier to catch the mouse this way, too. The Man With Long Pants thinks cleaning up my place is an important thing to do. I like him because I know I can tell him anything and he isn't going to judge me, like, I told him that I had so many dirty dishes that I had to wash them in the bathtub and he just said that was very resourceful. He says more important things, but mostly, I like to keep them between him and me.

OK so I just stepped outside and it feels like the first day of spring, although it is only February, but it's warm and sunny and smells wonderful—like clean trees! It feels like something good is coming and I'm actually kind of anxious to stay outside so I go back in and stare out my window and think of who to call. I could call my sister—I really could, I mean, it's not like I'm never going to talk to her again, and although I think I have it figured out, I still want to go over this mouse housing with her—but I'm not quite up for that. Sometimes I think she looks at me and sees our mother and that's not good because my sister is still very angry in those regards. So very, very hurt and angry.

I see my *Hey, neighbor* with an "A" walk into her apartment and think that if I could only remember her name, I'd ask her if she wants to go get something to eat, because you can't very well ask someone to eat with you if you don't know her name. I think for awhile until I come up with a *brilliant* plan and then I brush my teeth and comb my hair and powder out the shine on my nose. I walk across the hall and knock. Hey, neighbor, I say and I open up the organizer that my sister gave me about a year ago and take the cap off of my pen with my teeth. She says, Hi, Julia, really sweetly. I tell her that I think it's a good idea that we have each other's phone numbers, even though we are just across the hall from each other because this is a big city and you never know. She says that's a great idea. I rip off a piece of paper with my name and number and ask for hers. She says, Five, five, five, one, one, three, five. I say, OK so now how do you spell you first name? I say, I got your last name from your mailbox, but I just want to make sure I spell your first name right because I am a crummy speller (which I *am*), and I am using a pen. I show her my pen and she just looks at me. OK, I say, *A* ... She hesitates for a moment and then says, *M* ... I say, Uh, huh, and? *Y*, she says, and then she stops. *Y*? I ask. Mm hm, she says, *Y*. I say, OK, great. She says, Great. I say, See you later and she says, See you, and she starts to close the door. I stick my hand on the door and say, For some reason, I thought you spelled it with an *I*. She smiles a little and shuts the door the rest of the way. I walk back into my place and shut and lock my own door. Food can wait; it will probably start raining or sleeting out anyhow; that's how winter is here. Out of the corner of my eye I swear I see a small, charcoal colored streak cross my throw rug. My cats are both sleeping belly-up on the sofa and the white one twitches like she's dreaming.

I think the mouse suspects that something is up. She doesn't seem scared, just resigned to the fact that I will, very soon, catch her. Maybe she just needed some space from her friends or something, so she moved here. I'll figure out how to use this thing and then I'll start actively trying to "house" her. It's probably time that I take her somewhere else. I'm smart enough to know that sometimes we have to let go of what we hold onto, even if she feels a bit like family. Sometimes we have to wake up and choose to stay up, even when the sun sets early in the day, and all we have to look forward to is spring and all the wonderful morning light she brings. But sometimes, on the other hand, we have to really work to gather the strength to go somewhere brighter; because life calls for energy, and energy calls for life. Exhausting, truly.

I'm feeling pretty wiped out but just before I place my head upon the pillow between my kitties the phone rings. Hello? I say, loudly like I wasn't about to nap.

Hey, I hear. It's my sister, Charlotte.

Hey, I say back.

Listen, she says, and then nothing but quiet comes through the phone. Then I hear crying.

Don't cry, I say, partially because you're supposed to say this and partially because every time Charlotte cries I feel my insides turn into a brick wall, just for equilibrium.

How are you? she asks.

I'm fine, I say. I'm like stones inside, I think, but don't say.

Julia, she cries. How are you?

OK, I say.

She coughs then speaks: It's just that I really want you to get the key to those padlocks on the bars on your windows, she says. I can't sleep until you get that key. I can't sleep!

Well I can't sleep with you hassling me all the time, I say.

Well that's it, Julia! That's it! I don't want you to sleep because if there is a fire you won't be able to get out of your windows. Your apartment is a goddamn firetrap, Julia!

I yawn full-force into the phone. This is what stones inside can do to you—they can turn you stone-cold mean.

She cries harder and I hang up the phone. I don't know why I do what I do, but I just did it so whatever, I'll sleep it off.

Deep into the night, so deep it's almost morning, my doorbell rings. It's Charlotte.

Don't be angry, she says. She is holding two fire extinguishers—one full size, one half. If you have a cooking fire, she says, don't use water; use salt. A bag of white crystals dangles from her pocket.

I rub bunches of hours of sleep from my eyes and say, I don't know how to use that mouse trap.

I'll show you, she says, and comes inside. You did your dishes, she says.

I shrug, but I'm glad she noticed. She also notices the new picture I hung of our mother. Charlotte isn't one for hanging pictures.

This is new, she says and stares.

I don't tell her that our mother reminded me that I had that picture way down deep in my picture box. I'm afraid she'll think I'm crazy and who knows, maybe I am.

It turns out that I was right about the mouse temporary housing trap-condo thing. Charlotte walks me though it anyway. She holds it gently; she does that with breakable things.

You have to keep a fresh cracker in here, she says, and I say that I will.

When she leaves she touches the new picture and says, If she had had a sister, everything would be different. She wouldn't have done what she did.

I feel like something crumbles inside. *Kabang!* like a small explosion. I hug Charlotte from behind and plan to cry when she leaves. She was so sure of that statement when she said it; she didn't even waver. A sister would have saved our mother.

First thing in the morning I motivate and call my landlord. He tells me he'll drop the padlock key in my mailbox this afternoon.

You really should have reminded me sooner, he says.

I'm reminding you now, I say.

Going to the park seems like something I should do on this half-way sunny, pre-spring day, so I go. I buy a pack of butter crackers, the type with soft cheese on the side and a red stick to spread it, and I perch upon the wall of a fountain and watch people. I eat slowly, like a little thing, like a tiny, cunning, no-one-can-see-me.

I watch people walk: from bench to garbage, garbage to bench, fountain to fountain, friend to friend. I look down in the moment before someone catches my eye and I spread my cheese. When I feel those pangs begin, when I start to remember why I don't usually come here, to the park, to slouch alone on a fountain, I force myself to lift my head and look beyond the grass and slate and trees. There, I think: go straight a block; turn right; step lightly over the cracks in the sidewalk. In my mind I can see it: stop at the light; cross the street; turn right again, left; walk through the cobbled section, and there, at the end, walk inside and there will be Charlotte. There, I think again when the pangs start up: go straight a block; turn right; step lightly over the cracks in the sidewalk…

And then I hear this: Hello, Julia.

Oh hello, I say, even before my eyes lift.

It's me, I hear her say, and then I see.

Hey neighbor, I say. Hey Amy. Hey.

You're sitting in the park? she says. I mean—

Yes, I say. It's a nice day.

I mean, she says, it's a nice day to sit in the park.

Yes, I say.

She tells me that she is on her way to work, but maybe sometime, she says, we can meet out here for lunch.

OK, I say. Let's do that someday soon.

OK, she says and smiles, really sweetly.

I take a cracker from my pack, then, and spread it with cheese. I hand it to her and she looks at it. I expect her to wave it away. Cheese crackers aren't the sort of things people who don't really know you accept. But then she takes it in her hand, and then she brings it to her mouth.

Thank you, she says. And then she eats it.

My sister, I hear myself say, lives down there, around the block—. I hear myself list the names of the streets: Chestnut, Walnut, Locust…

All trees, Amy says.

All trees, I say. She smiles and says she's late for work so she'd better go. She waves as she walks and I wave back pretty hard—not so hard that she thinks I'm strange, but just hard enough that someone sitting on some bench might take notice.

It's amazing how small things can trigger a true commencement. Case in point: the following day the mouse moves easily into her temporary home. The door closes behind her and she seems to think nothing but, Oh fantastic! Crackers! The kitties watch her sniff around this strange new place and I swear they look a little sad. Part of me thinks I should keep her for a little longer, but I know that's not right. I know that this is my home and I need to make some room for me in it.

I decide to take her some place right away. I don't care if I get rained on later; right now it's half-way sunny and I'll take advantage of that. I walk for sometime until I feel the breeze of my mother touch my hair, which is when I look up. What I see is the spot where I will release my mouse— it's under a knotted maple tree by the Schuylkill River. I sit on an old bench and really check it out. I think it's right because there are two gothic teenagers having a picnic there. How can the two Goths be so darkly lovely? They both wear capes and shiny black boots and dark lipstick. She has burgundy hair and his is black. They are pale as fright and they're eating out of brown lunch bags, which cracks me the hell up! It's like light and dark all mixed up and turned around—day and night; sun and moon; evil and good; gothic and picnic. They eat apples, too. How funny things are, sometimes.

The wind is cold here, but the sun is warm. The Canadian Geese (who no longer migrate because their magnetic pull to the earth, which gives them a sense of direction, is all screwed up because of urban sprawl and cellular phones and things) aren't really messing around this far down the river, so that shouldn't be an issue. I think she'll really like it here, by the muddy river. When the Goths leave I plan to put her down directly where they sat. I close my eyes and picture her eating through her final cracker, her thin, naked hands will grip the tasty crumbs as she decides whether she should stay or go. *Choose.* And then she'll decide and I'll see her head out alongside the ways of the water—running in a cool streak over the sun-struck stones and the swells of the earth and in between the trees that hover over this river—this deep, thick river that takes all the unwanted things out of this wonderful city I'm trying to live in.

the tree that took brooke's faith away

It stood thick up from the bottom of the hill; from on top it looked no smaller, just lost within its grandeur. Brooke wrapped her fists around the rope some long-gone kid once tied around a branch. The twins, below—two boys well-known for mooning cheeks against their bedroom window, tossing underwear in the street for laughs—looked up at her and said: "Jump off the hill!"

She *would*, she said. The thing was, though, she couldn't shake the image of that dead dog she had found inside the black trash bag she thought could be first base, right before the twins said, Screw the game, let's swing. The thing was, though, she didn't know just when the dog had died, before—or god forbid—while within the twist-tied bag.

The twin boys laughed and waved their arms. Brooke saw they had a grown-up thing like interest spark inside their eyes. She knew her hair hung pale and wave-less. She knew she had a certain sort of swooping in her spine. She knew these boys, they saw these things. The dog, she thought, and when he died—they didn't understand.

But it was dead. This she knew. And here she stood, so head to head with this grand tree. *I should swing,* she thought. *I should run down the hill, clutch the rope, and swing like tether ball around the trunk.* The dog lay buried, now, where short-stops stood, and on its mound—the dirt now ruddy, upside-downed by her digging hands—she knew she placed one fist of stones she'd gathered by the old train tracks.

The boys cried: "Jump!"

The bag had been half-veiled in leaves. She thought it could be a fine first base. She thought at first it was filled with soil—it had that heavy feel of something from which trees and flowers sprung.

"Jump already! *Jump!*"

Brooke gripped the rope. *Who killed the dog?* The tree stood thick, went and up and up and up. The twins, they stared, way up, and up and up; and then Brooke feared—*where were the other baseball players? Where was the catcher? Where's the ump?*—she ran and parted ways with land. *Who killed the dog? Who tied the bag?* She soared and swung right down the hill, around the tree, toward the tree, toward the boys. She thought: He should have used his teeth. She thought: He should have fought and fought and fought. She thought: I think I know where next things go. I see it clearly from up here. And by the *here* she meant just where the pause occurred. Before descent, before the jealous world would grab at her right from the very pits of its so very needy core.

how to best say goodbye to a very old house

When my father moved, we thought the earth would shake. We thought the house would boom and tremble and the winds whip wildly around. We thought his neck would strain and redden if we dropped a load of books. We thought he'd quickly empty every room in a rushed up frenzy, *Get it out! Get it out!* We waited for the freaked out exit and the slamming doors and the reasons why we all knew well, because our father loved it, oh how he loved that house.

He loved the old light fixtures, the paint chipped doors, the full of creak stairs, the splintered up floors and walls with peeled-down paper, the way the water loses heat, the fireplaces, basement stairs, the newspapers in the deacon's bench. My father loved them so. So much so that he stayed for years—for ten, for twenty, then a few more after. He stayed when I was sweet and four and welcomed my baby sister when she was carried through the door in my mother's arms, both wrapped in red. My sign upside down—upright it read—*Welcome home brand new baby!* And a photo of it he keeps in his drawer of keepsakes—the light from outside shining in past my mother, flickered through the oak trees in little spits on the ground.

He stayed when we grew and our mother moved out and the sofa was gone. The chairs were all missing and the floors were all bare and the kitchen was quiet all day and all night.

But he stayed and read papers in the early morning sun and he slept by the window where the curtains had been and he loved counting steps from one floor to the next, because, with no doubt, he really loved that house.

So when, with his new wife, he decided to move, my sisters and I feared the worst of the bad. We thought things would fly and his heart would give out. We thought he would hide his deep love for that house but instead he moved smoothly from one floor to the next. He held the old banister as he swung up the steps. He lifted his books and rocked on the loose floorboards and he knew the old creaks and the rusted hinge squeaks of the doors on the closets. We watched as he moved from one floor to the next. Let me show you, he said, how to best say goodbye to a very old house.

He walked up the stairs and ran his dry fingers on the crack in the wall. He stood in the hallway; he leaned into the room where the old ghost made his home. The window was open just a wide enough crack for the ghost to move in and out of that empty, back room. Invite the ghost to come, he said, or invite him to stay for the next family. Move over to these doors where the balcony is. Bang the stiff bolt with the palm of your hand. Walk out and feel the cool autumn day. Brush some leaves with your foot. Look down at the station. Hear the deep, subtle rumble of the approaching train. Hear the scream of the tracks as it comes to a halt. Look at the conductor leaning out of his window. Cup your hands around your mouth. *Honk your horn!* you should yell, *Honk your horn!* Now, one last time watch as the man pulls the rope and hear the sounding of the horn, sad and long, like an animal, out of place and alone.

highway kind

I called him Ant-nee. He wore a snake of plastic vein within his arm to save his kidney. He and I, we sculpted plants. He had a way with succulents; did the driving to the homes needing beauty. Along the way he'd stop for men along the median, give them dollars, search their eyes. I asked him why for every one. I joked and said his karma was clear by now. He turned the radio up, gunned the engine, said, Who knows which one might be my Pop? One day, he said. One day I'll see mine eyes in his.

the hills in pittsburgh are so steep they sometimes turn to stairs

Cousin Dave had a snake and Kirsty loved the snake. I can't remember what sort of snake but I know it was a boy snake and when I shut my eyes and look for it in my head, I see a python, thick as thighs. It was really his friend Downtown's snake, but he kept it in Cousin Dave's room and Kirsty was always in there, petting and stroking the big snake. Cousin Dave was called Cousin Dave because he was Markus's cousin, and we all knew Markus first. Downtown got his name from drinking liquid acid. I can't tell you how his name and the acid connect; I just know that they do.

Kirsty liked to watch the snake get fed, but I was always telling him, Cousin, don't let me see the mice you feed that snake; I do not want to see them ever. He called me a prude and I informed him that it made no sense and he just said, Yuh-huh it does. Cousin Dave was sweet like that and jumpy, too, so I usually cleared my throat before walking into his room and asking for some weed or looking for Kirsty. We smoked quite a lot of weed back then; the living room had zero windows, so it was sort of necessary. I drew a window with markers on the wall once, but it wasn't the same. Everyone liked it, though—Cousin Dave, Downtown, Markus, Kirsty, Nikita, Joel, and Money Cris all said it was a great window; and when we had parties with the punks and the white skinz and the black skinz and that one gay, half-black, half-Jewish skin, everyone made comments about the window. I hung yellow curtains on it and everything. We threw great parties. Did you know that beer brings out roaches? Well it does. Did you know that drinking a half bottle of liquid peroxide will not kill you or make you pass out, but will probably turn your poo green and too soft to hold in? Truth. Ask Money Cris who crashed with us until he was officially moved in rent-free, and who was prone to moments of such high drama that he made discoveries like that all of the time. Go ahead and ask him. He's the guy wanting to crash on your sofa who steals your cigarettes and who totes a spider web on his elbow.

Cousin Dave was not real partial to Money Cris. As I said, Cousin Dave was jumpy and Money Cris had a way of storming into situations. Money Cris didn't like the snake, either, or at least he didn't like how much *hush-hush* time Kirsty spent with the snake in Cousin Dave's room. There was some tension there, all right. Kirsty just said, *Shh,* and everyone was supposed to look away and keep quiet I guess. When Money Cris got angry, I got scared and said, I hate that snake, and Kirsty said, Don't blame the snake. *Shh.*

Which was when I made the executive decision to let Kirsty hit rock bottom before I would help her get her shit together. The problem is rock bottom is not always where it seems to be. Sometimes rock bottom might look like a girl with big, quiet eyes who is starting to bulge in the middle, who smokes cigarette after cigarette and holds a restraining order against the supposed baby's daddy, Money Cris; but sometimes, that is just the false bottom, like the false summit on a mountain, only the mountain is turned upside down and shoved in the ass of earth.

Sometimes the true rock bottom appears late, late at night, so late that it is almost morning, and the girl with the bulging stomach finds some sort of true solace on the floor of the bathroom, *shh*—her stomach filled with so much chaos, that chaos cracks the egg open and spills it red onto the tiled floor. Sometimes true rock bottom appears in the form of a thick snake curled up in the tub to keep the girl company as she goes and loses everything. And sometimes true rock bottom is only discovered because Cousin Dave really truly loved that snake and wondered where he had slithered off to, and wondered if he was frightened, or sad, or hungry, or just feeling like there is no point left to life—feeling like there is nothing to strive for but down, down, down.

flowing, flown

In the field stands a jealous man with fifteen eyes stored
inside the cuffs of well-worn khaki pants. His pockets pull
with clinking dimes and when his hand jams in the silver-
dipped copper disks clank and gather. Ten cents per, he
says, and *pop!* he buys another eye, and *slide*, he lines it in
the folds, for no one looks for gems on ankles, gems tucked
in a rolled-up sleeve. He likes the way they pulse and blink
and try to hear by straining wide. He'd like to buy up every
one; he'd like to fill the air between his thumb and finger;
finger, ring; ring and pinky; he'd like to walk with
outstretched hands to see how things appear from there.

He spies a little side-eyed bird and tries to buy his two for one;
but no, this bird won't sell: I have no use for dimes, he says. But,
clink, the man jams in his hand. Two dimes for one—the bird
says no. Four dimes for one—the bird says no. Ten dimes for
one—the bird says no; and when he bends his wings for flight
the man throws all those copper disks, but *soft* they slide inside
the layered feathers on those wings. The man grabs in his fist the
eyes that blink and strain inside those khaki folds. *Swoosh, zip!*
But *soft*, they roll upon those wings; they roll off onto air and
flutter there, tears welling up because of wind. The man says,
Nice to know how things appear. He's jealous of their height,
their lonely sense of wonder what, and where to go from here.

dead dog rising

My father has not slept with any sort of confidence in over one and one-half weeks. The dog is dying, see; he's dying in that pacing way. He's thin and gray and moving like he has big plans—the kind that wake him in the night to say, *Let's go! Let's break away!*

His claws have grown and since his pads are wasting, sucked-in, sunken soles, claws tap the floor, they keep the time. *Click clack. Click clack. Click.* That sound there—that back and forth—is what wakes my father and drives him mad. *Click clack*, he tells me, then *skid*, then sometimes, *thump*—which means the dog has lost it.

My father keeps a baseball bat for just this kind of thing, for if the night should make a sound—*creak, slam, shattering glass*. He'll grab that bat and head downstairs, so angry then, more so than scared. *Get out! Get out of my stone house!*

He gives the dog some Valium. He pushes down on his thin backside. He looks him in the eyes and says, *You know me, Dog. I know you know me.* The dog has made such big, big plans and hasn't got the time.

He rises later in the night. *Click clack*, he walks. *Click clack. Click.*

My father, now mad with sleep, or lack of it, or simply clouded, grabs the bat in his rough, dry fist. *Creak, shuffle, ominous thump.* He runs downstairs in panic, fury. He is angry at the nighttime sounds. He holds the bat above his head. *Get out! Get out of my stone house!*

The dog is there, on sorry legs, with sorry claws. He looks toward the man, the bat, and says, *You know me, Man. I know you know me.*

to the woman who sat
with her back to the door

Such a curious smell in the air tonight: part skunk, part
fire, part rubber of your tire, pulled liquid hot across
that road.

I told you once to turn around. I didn't like the way you sat.

I have very little to say to you. Your brother is an asshole,
one. Your ukelele's heading south, that would be two. And
three, three would be the jogger only broke his legs.

I *think* I told you to turn around. It's not safe to sit with
your back to the door.

I had very little to say to you.

Your shoes he strew all over the sidewalk. Your books
and clothing, too.

Such an asshole, coming to clean you out and taking the
subway there to do it. He had no intention of saving you, I
mean saving your things, I mean doing with them something
with some class.

Why this smell of skunk and fire?

Motorcycle tires have an oily coat until a certain mile; at
something like ten you saw that jogger. Well, good for you
for breaking his legs. They'll heal and he will walk again.
Oh, four, I gave the amps back to the kid downstairs. He
almost lost his dog one night to a hit and run. *I'm so sorry*,
he kept wailing, *I'm so sorry, are you hurt?* To love anything
that much is dumb. He could have been bleeding inside,

one organ drowning all the others as the kid slept off his beer and waited until the morning to take the dog to the vet.

I'm so sorry, I'm so sorry. Are you hurt?

Don't sit like that, goddamn it, it's just not safe! I could open up the door and knife you in the back, and if I *could* do it, then think of all who *would?*

she let her hair go nuts
unless there was a party

Perhaps that was why they wrote:
Dear Ms.

Please come to the office of Homeland Security by noon Thursday, the 5th of this month. We are located in San Antonio, Texas, an hour or so from your home. Call for directions. Please note the fact that your green card will not be renewed if you fail to appear.

She brought a friend for the drive, which was not far, but *unlovely*, and therefore she welcomed distraction. Philip wore loads of black hair for his beard, which often looked bogus, and she thought: How funny if they choose to shake him down for it. This was her humor. It was Irish, at heart, with a healthy dose of Australian snuck in. Hers had been a family that traveled. Until the day her father drowned while swimming laps in the ocean, she was hither and thither all the time.

The officers were pleasant enough, but made no effort to apologize.

My hair has gone nuts, she said. But unless you're throwing a party I am sorry but it'll have to do. Your letter, she added, it mentioned something about bio-testing me. Is this what you're now doing?

I'm simply filling in paper work, Ma'am, the man said.

Ah, she said. I figured as much. One should think bio-testing would sting just a little.

One should think, he said.

She asked if they would pay for her day of missed work, but the man wouldn't answer.

Even in Ireland, she said, I was pulled off the plane before we got to the gates. It was my fault, of course; I had wrongly assumed I was visiting *home*.

Why are you here? The man asked, looking down.

Well I got your letter, you see.

He looked up, squinted his eyes.

She just smiled.

It's time for the test, the man said, and then he led her down the hall to another, taller man.

Her friend Philip stood and waved through the glass partition between them. *I'm here,* he mouthed. *I'll stay right here.*

The taller man stared at him. Your friend, he said. He has the look of a suspect.

Shake him down, she said, and laughed. I'm kidding, of course. His hair simply grows like that.

And yours? The man asked, and gestured to the wires, led her into the room.

Are we having a party? she asked. Well then, it'll do.

too huge

I made a request of no crying, for I had the grand task of handling the cat.

No crying, I said. Do whatever it takes to wait until I've gone.

He agreed to blame his contact lenses and to leave once I'd passed through security, but not before. Just in case the cat didn't fly.

This cat can fly, I said. He will.

Like a superhero, he said. The sort of comment I could count on him for.

I said "this cat" to avoid saying "our" or "my." *That* dog looks concerned. I had said this earlier as I stacked my bags by the door of *that* home. Don't forget to water *that* plant. *This* street is still asleep.

These neighbors haven't woken yet, he said.

I looked at him and snort-laughed, swallowed stones.

The cat curled drugged and dense inside the fabric carrier. I sought to bring him on the plane surreptitiously, to avoid explaining the fact of him. It could lead to talk of my one-way ticket. It costs eighty dollars each way to carry him aboard. Someone might say that up and back costs a pretty penny, and then what? I'd have to correct them. No no, just *up*. Then the panic might set in.

* * *

I was ready when the wide-belted woman by the metal walkthrough hollered that I must remove the animal from the carrier and walk him through. I had thought ahead and worn white because I knew I'd have to hold the great fluff to my chest. I unzipped the bag and glanced over to my husband, who fooled with his contacts on the other side of the security lines, rubbing and blinking his eyes. I looked forward to pressing the soft whiteness to my chest. I planned to push him hard into my solar plexus to keep that hot swell down.

I pulled him out of the bag. It was snug on him. It was as if he *wore* the bag more than the bag *held* him. For a week I'd take a measuring tape to his hugeness as he slept, willed him to lose some length, some girth. He was supposed to be able to stand up and move around in there, but come on, what good's a cat so small he can turn around in 16x9x10? Besides, I knew his ways and his ways were not that active, so I bought the bag and told him to hunker down for a few hours. Catch some Z's, I said.

I clutched him into my chest. I thought of ten years earlier when we found him in the basement of a highrise in which our friends lived—our friends who were a "one-cat couple," they said, when they were still a couple—and whose one cat used the toilet and fetched the paper from the hallway, no lie. I thought these friends were the sort to look up to. I had slipped the gray kitten inside my coat and we walked the ten blocks home and thought of names for it. My husband suggested Concrete or Slate, but after we washed him we started to lean more toward the clean and banal, like Cotton or Snow. I pressed my face down into the cat's nape when I thought of this time, and when I thought of the name on which we had finally settled—the name of the month in which we had met; the month in which we had married. That cat was like a calendar. Friends teased us by mixing it up, calling him January, September, ridiculous months like July.

The detector buzzed when we crossed under. The wide-belted woman ran a wand over me—my front, my back—and then over the cat—his collar, my left hand holding the softness under his arms, where my ring shone through his downy fur. I knew it was his ID tag that did it, but how appropriate, I thought, if the ring had sounded an alarm.

All right, she said. Let's see him in action.

Did she want him to dance? I bounced him and then stopped. He's not a big performer, I said.

Put him in the carrier, please.

It's regulation, I said, leaning over and using the cat's paw to point to the tag that said, Compliant with Aviation Standards.

I'm checking the fit, Ma'am. Place the animal inside the case.

I looked over toward where my husband stood, but couldn't see his face through the people in line. I caught sight of a bit of his shoulder, though, and wanted desperately to tap it, say, What of the fit? How many points off for an ill fit? He'd know. It's the sort of thing I could always count on him for.

Ma'am, she said. Place the animal inside.

I held the bag beneath the cat's rear; his rear that slung like a potato sack due to the sedative. Why was I here? Why was I taking our cat?—my cat, that cat? Why had we decided this was the way? Every morning the cat waited to eat until the dog was ready. Who would he wait for now? We had no children, we had decided, so now's the time to separate, reassess our situation for a year or so.

If ever there's a time.

It was the *or so* that killed me. It woke me at night. Me and that cat, shoving his nose into my eye telling me to wake up already.

The cat's arms stuck straight out as I slipped the bag over his enormity. I tucked his paws inside, zipped the front. I shook the bag as if he might settle into some mysterious crevice, make some room for him in there.

Nuh-uh, the wide-belted woman said. She shook her head. Her eyes wide like saucers.

He likes to be contained, I said, and pushed the palms of my hands together to show what? To show, *held together.* To show, *held.*

Nuh-uh, she said again.

To show, *Please.*

I felt a thumping in my chest. I looked over to my husband, who had committed to the parting, who said the pain of the very moment of leaving would subside, yet the continuation of stagnation would last forever.

I had asked him if he might graph that for me.

Now I saw him rubbing his nose as if it had wronged him

You got someone who can take this cat?

What? I asked.

You got someone—

I can take him, I said. This cat can fly. Like a superhero, I added.

This cat can't fly, she said. This cat too huge—

He likes to be *contained*, I said.

This cat *too huge* to fly. She shook her head, reached for the cat that slept so unaware inside his carrier. You got someone—

I got someone, I said. I do, but when I looked he seemed so far away I said, He'll never reach! And what I meant was that his body—so hunkered now and shaking—it could never reach out and grab the cat that couldn't fly. Not unless I threw the cat, or left the line and started over. Not unless I missed my flight and stayed instead within stagnation. We're young, we said. We have no children. Now's the time.

Now's the time, I said to her. The cat is fine. He likes to be *contained.*

He ain't happy in there, she said.

What's *happy?* I said. Nothing's *happy.* Nothing's more

or less OK with what they've got, and what we've got is quite OK. It's really very much OK.

OK ain't compliant, she said.

She grabbed the handles of the carrier, started to lift him somewhere different.

You'll see it when you return, she said.

It's a one-way! I said, maybe shouted, waved my boarding pass.

Ma'am, this is not the place to lose it. She held the cat up, away from me and headed for the place where confiscated items went.

I looked toward my husband. I caught a wisp of hair and what seemed to be his hand upon it. Is *OK* fine? I wanted to ask. Is OK perhaps the final goal? Where might *familiar* factor in? Where might: *we like the same ice cream.* Where might: *I know you.*

I grabbed at him, the cat inside the carrier. I grabbed at him and said, Don't take him from me!

Ma'am! she said with some conviction, although she looked away from me, toward another, who locked me then within his eyes as he walked forward. *Is there a situation here?*

Yes, I thought. No, I said. My husband by now had noticed the hold-up and had maneuvered himself into a position of receiving the cat over the black zip-line. I saw this in slow motion and something burst behind my rib cage; as it did my body filled with dense, hot liquid that added weight, that gave me a gelatinous pull upon the earth. I felt too heavy to move toward gate 34, let alone to lift up off the ground and fly to the place I had previously thought of as home, where my new life—temporal, *or so*—awaited my landing.

Hands guided me away from the security line and I heard myself tell the wide-belted woman of the cat hole my mother had so kindly cut into her basement door, and now for what? I looked back at my husband, saw the weight in the bag tipped him to the left. His eyes looked very sorry. He stretched open the palm of his free hand to show, what? To show he had nothing. I envied that cat. I, too, felt too huge to fly. I wanted to be contained. Just reach for me. Grab for me over the zip-line.

When we planned the wedding nearly a decade before, I had argued with the caterer because he insisted we provide more main dish choices than we had wanted to.

We're not looking to feed these people for the entire weekend, I had said. We're young and can't afford it. I looked at the man who would soon be my husband, and he agreed, although he did so non-committed-like, with a nod and shrug of his shoulders. *Who are you people?* I thought then of men.

Perhaps you should wait until you're older, the caterer suggested, until you can do it correctly.

I felt defiance well up within me. Had I not been doing it for love I would have married out of spite at that moment; but later I remember waking at night and thinking of it, only in my half-sleep state I heard the caterer grumble that it's a long *life*—not a long *reception*—and people get hungry.

Perhaps you should wait until you're older then. Until you can do it correctly.

My husband had turned away by now. He walked with that cat slung in that bag toward the exit door of the airport. We're still young, I thought, as I saw the lovely leanness of my husband's waist, as I slid my own weighted legs over the slick terrazzo, toward gate 34.

There once had been a superhero doll weighted just like this, his rubber arms filled with a gelatinous goo that stretched when you pulled and reformed when you let go. If you pierced the skin with scissors it would leak. What was he called, that heavy, stretchy superhero? He wasn't the caped sort—he was earth-bound and tortured. He did good things reluctantly, not due to bravery. It hurt his body to do what needed to be done. It ripped his clothes and made him feel very much alone. What was he called?

He would know the answer, I thought. As I pulled my weighted legs over shiny terrazzo and walked passed the twenties, toward the mid-thirties, I made a mental note to ask him about this later. We're from the same time and all— he and I. For years we had counted on the other for just this sort of vital, vital, vital thing.

flutter in night

Have you heard this yet? The daughter flew home to care for the mother, whose pump is still tick ticking—though now with aid—which means she leaves the kitchen when the microwave clicks on. She holds her heart, as if to pray—one spotted hand placed on the next as she backs out on slippered feet, head bowed toward this new-world oven. She knows that time has won.

Have you seen her yet? The daughter, too, is aging with the grace of black-faced geese—those velvet-necked birds that foot-flit around the river who refuse to move for anyone. She often jogs by—shuffles her too-big feet and holds her arms bent near her face, a little like a fighter might. The geese just glance, then look away, fearing nothing from this sweet old bird or from the dust she's just kicked up.

These rounded, dense, migrating geese know a thing or two about time passing. They know that on their way to Canada they feel the tug of earth's great magnet grow strong around this Cooper River, and though New Jersey is not quite right, it is a place to pass the time. It is a place to rest until the sun will set one hour sooner than it did the day they landed. At night they'll study the pattern of stars—great necks extended, pointing up toward the blackened sky through which they'll fly until this time next year, and that time the other, and all those nights placed in between.

Has she told you yet? The old mother would like to fly home to New Scotland one final time; she'd like to catch a strong tail wind and float above what doesn't count. She'd land when air is smelling right and let the cold do what it will, as she lay down in a frozen field: her body done, her old pump tuckered, her daughter flying on her own by mapping stars and galaxies when, by night, she carries on.

heists

The neighbor said he *saw* Charlie give the guns to that writer.

You didn't *see* it, Charlie Junior said, because it didn't *happen*. That writer *stole* those guns from the cabin and furthermore, he left coffee rings on the counter and *furthermore*, all his movies are about what? What are they about?

I've never *seen* his movies, the neighbor said.

Heists! Charlie Junior said, and then he slammed the phone down.

Charlie Junior's daughter had driven from her home to his for a visit and she suggested that *she* spend some time in Vermont that coming year, fix the old cabin up, live in it for awhile and eventually rent it weekly to people with money.

Vacationers, she said. You'll make more than you would with a full-time tenant like that writer was.

Furthermore, he said, his hand pounding the table, which made his daughter startle, I *sent* that writer many letters about those guns after Charlie died.

And? his daughter asked.

And nothing! he shouted.

Maybe Charlie *did* give them to him—

Quiet! he shouted. You're just like those characters in his movies, always interrupting everyone for no good reason.

I've seen them, he said. Fatalistic, interrupting *heist*-flicks. With *weird* enunciations. Enunciations! Not *once* does a character die in a way that that writer should die!

You're really angry, the daughter said.

Those are *my* guns! Charlie should have given them to *me*! And those goddamn coffee rings.

She thought: *Coffee is for closers*, and other lines from that writer's movies. *Maple syrup grows on trees.* She laughed at the thought, those stunning trees in Vermont that she would love to see again. Maybe she could turn the place into a bed and breakfast. She'd use the name of that writer to promote it.

What? Charlie Junior said. You don't think a son should inherit his father's favorite guns? Well you and that writer, then, you can *both* go to hell!

But he had so many guns, she said. I remember them—I remember them and how they lined the bathtub, how they stacked upon the sofa. There were so many how do you know which ones were his favorites?

Because they're the ones that *writer* has, he said. They're the ones the neighbor saw Charlie give to him! And *furthermore*, he said, who with money would want to vacation in a cabin painted like fall foliage? It's an insane asylum! I'm writing a letter, he said. This isn't over. I'm telling that writer he can *have* the damn cabin! I'm giving it to him, guns and all. Case closed.

But wait, the daughter said, shouldn't I be the one to have—

Quiet! he shouted. You're just like those characters in his movies—always interrupting everyone for no good reason.

losing the red house

The heat has always been cruel to me, and so in a way, if it were hot, I would have been expecting it. But it wasn't hot. It wasn't even sunny. It was cold and gray and there were ice crystals decorating the bare tree limbs and those trees glistened with such glory that the thought of them, even now, makes my heart thump thump so I can feel it in my chest. If someone had told me I could lose it during a time like that in a place like Vermont, I'd have told him he didn't know me; he didn't know me and he didn't know my true, deep love of that place.

My brother built the cabin over twenty-five years ago during a manic period when all was right in his world as long as he was there, in Lake Elmore, Vermont; he sold it to me ten years later when he finally came down and headed south to become a Baptist. He had collected three junker cars in the driveway and I got rid of all but one that would give the place the look of someone living there even when we weren't. My wife Caroline and I drove up from our home in Philadelphia any chance we could and over the years that added up to quite some time that we spent in the Red House. Our neighbor, Johnny Gillion, took good care of the place and I always enjoyed seeing him look up from his wood chopping to give us a wave every time we pulled on up that snow covered drive. At the bottom of the drive lived Warren

Judson and his wife, Alverta, and we'd often pass them on the dirt road walking their dog, Chainsaw. Like true Vermonters, they'd simply nod their heads and say hello as if they had just seen us that morning, even when we hadn't made the eight-hour trip for over six weeks.

Warren was the owner of the Elmore General Store and he was also the Fire Marshall, so he was a good neighbor to know. They were all good neighbors to know. Gillion was a science teacher and a piano player and a bit of a legend in the town for playing sad songs in a local pub. His wife died of cancer about five years before we bought the house and so it was just him and his son and their crazy dog, Sundance, living next door. Caroline's mother and aunt had both died of breast cancer and the very mention of the disease brought back the vacancy she felt inside without them, and so she often invited the Gillions over for supper, thinking that they too must have suffered with that gaping black hole.

Not too long ago, Caroline had had a breast lumpectomy herself, and now lived in a perpetual state of detecting; always cupping what remained, loveless, as if she was training herself to live without them altogether. She could be cold when cold was called for, yet she was kind and warm as springtime to Johnny and his son. I enjoyed seeing his son, Franklin, as he was nearly the same age as my son Jesse who lived in New Jersey with his mother.

Sometimes, after the meal, we'd share some duty-free Scotch from the Canadian border and sit and listen to the wood snap in the stove. "Come on over and take some of my orange wood," is what Gillion would always say at the end of the night, and so we'd tromp across the drive to his shed—Franklin practically sleep walking—and he'd fill my wood sack with some sweet smelling logs that he said would crackle through the night. I never turned down his offers of wood because I know well when someone has something that they feel good about doing—not out of debt or obligation, but simply out of kindness.

Gillion was also the head of the reservoir committee. The reservoir provided all of us who lived on Softwood Road with water. There was some joking early on, when we first started coming up to the cabin, that the Judsons always knew when Caroline and I had come up, because their water pressure would drop considerably. That's how things were around there, just like that. Just like life and everything in it was no big deal. I believe it had to do with the snow and the ice and the bone chilling cold—things no man, no Fire Marshall, no reservoir committee head or general store manager could do anything about. That land was at will of the woods, the beasts on the mountains, and the wind that whipped-on through.

Things began to go badly for me at work in the city. I couldn't stand the click clack of all the computer keys around me. I hated the hum of the central heating system. I felt a rage boiling up from within every time I saw the heading, *Memorandum*. Each week it seemed I brought home a migraine and went to bed without a word to Caroline. Our marriage suffered; it was my second marriage and it began to feel very much like my first. I felt myself slipping backwards, as if on ice, into what my life was before I met Caroline, and the only part of that life I wanted to remember was my son. I had decided some time before that Jesse deserved a father who stood tall on solid ground. I had to do something, and so I made arrangements with my office to work from home, Caroline quit her secretarial position, and we moved our world up to Vermont to spend the winter of that year. Although Caroline had expressed some unease about being far from her doctor, she agreed that it was the right decision when we woke on that first morning and heard the noiseless sound of snow falling onto itself upon the dirt road, our red roof, and the bottom corner of our bedroom window. Caroline moved into my arms and there she remained. I felt at home and at peace for the first time in quite awhile. Jesse often called to get a snow report and we made plans for him to spend some time with us. Jesse asked if we could ice fish when he got there and I told him I couldn't think of anything more exciting, which was about the greatest truth I have uttered to this day. Weeks went by and Caroline and I grew more and more calm and in love and at home in Lake Elmore.

I spent some time every morning with a cup of coffee, standing on our front porch taking all of that beauty in. Caroline would be in the bath and that would be our time alone for the day. Through the bare-bone trees, I began to see Warren Judson walk up Gillion's drive at that same time every morning. I'd give him a silent wave and he'd smile and wave back and that would be that. I assumed he was talking to Gillion about some town issues, and secretly, I felt a bit envious to not be included in the committees. Caroline convinced me that they all considered us true neighbors and that I had every right to attend the meetings and maybe even join a committee. I thought I would discuss it with Gillion and so one day soon after that, Caroline walked over to his house and invited him to supper.

Johnny and Franklin came over shortly after that and we shared a meal and talked about the wonderful cold we were experiencing that winter. We sat by the wood stove and drank some duty-free, as we came to simply call it, and I was preparing to bring up the subject of committees when Gillion told me that there had been some complaints about our using the reservoir. "Complaints?" I asked him. "By whom?" He wouldn't tell me names but I figured out that it had to be Warren Judson complaining about his water pressure. I felt my neck turn red when I realized that he had been walking up Gillion's drive in the mornings during Caroline's bath. Gillion told me that it was only right that I should provide our own tank in the basement or else dig our own well for our own private water source. I told him that we just couldn't keep a tank in the basement because we would be gone for weeks at a time and would not be able to keep it clean. "I have a son down there, you know," I told him. "You might have a problem with rodents dying in there," he said, and that was why he suggested digging our own well, which would cost a lot of money. Then he added that he thought it was about time that we got rid of the old junker car in the driveway, too.

I couldn't believe what I was hearing. I didn't bring up the town meetings. I didn't tell him that I loved Elmore and everything about it and that I felt like it was truly my home, even though I still had a life to contend with some states south. I wanted to tell him how the cold helped my blood to flow and kept my head from pounding and throbbing. I felt a dug-out hole inside that I hadn't felt before. Gillion looked at his son and said that he had fallen asleep by the fire and so that was his cue to head back home. He left without offering me any orange wood.

Caroline remained silent as I poured myself a few shots of the duty-free. She was good about knowing when the talking should wait until the next day. We made our way silently up to bed and I fell asleep easily, due only to the scotch in my blood, keeping it thin.

I woke to Caroline shaking me. "That noise," she said, "what is it? Do you hear it?" I opened my eyes and held my breath and listened. I heard a low, echoed groan that came from a deep and dark place—a well or a damp cave. I heard a sound like a horse—a giant of a horse—shaking its head and snorting out through its long snout. "It's a bull moose," I said, and I listened to the heavy steps crunching through the frozen ground. Caroline said that it sounded as if it could knock the wall in and I told her I wouldn't be surprised if it could. I said that a home may appear to be a fortress until it is confronted by something of that magnitude, and then you see that it is nothing but some old wood and nails that could split apart like something that was only meant to be temporary. All of this was almost not spoken, but breathed into each other in a way that no one else would be able to understand. Caroline curled up into my arms and for a few moments we were silent while the moose considered our home. Then, softly, she told me that she had found something earlier that day and I shut my eyes tight when she said the words *breast* and *lump* and *back home to the city.* I didn't tell her that we *were* home. I only held her and strained my ears to hear the bull moose as he considered heading back into the frigid woods, his hoofs puncturing packed snow as he rounded a corner of the Red House.

this, about the man i met in nearly nowhere

Out here in nearly nowhere I met this man. About him I know something something, and no one can tell me otherwise. The man was out in nearly nowhere, so how chance a thing like meeting. Out here one loses track of somewhere when all this nowhere nearly looms.

About this man, he chooses flight if such an option options through. Out here wings float on wind as if there's nowhere else but here in nearly nowhere; out here in nearly nowhere where I met this man who nowheres with me, with—or even so—*without* the wings we both will choose if such an option options through out here in nearly nowhere.

janey at the door

I sat in Benny's room—a simple, square section of our home that he called his office—and waited for the doorbell to ring. I knew it would ring and I waited. I had just made up my mind completely, one-hundred percent certainly, to leave Benny. I couldn't do it any more—no bones about it.

Janey would ring the bell. Her timing was always so terrifically poor that I just knew she would come ringing at any minute. Janey's husband was a drunk and he was ugly so I tried very hard to be kind to her.

The doorbell rang. I held my breath and it rang again. I stayed where I sat, on one of Benny's five desks. *For the love of God, who needs five desks?* The doorbell rang again and again and again, although this last time it kept ringing—she just kept her finger there—not buzz buzz buzz, but one long, oscillating wail. The weight of the world was on that bell and I felt compelled to rescue it. I ran down the stairs and answered the door.

"Janey," I said, "this is not a good time."

"When is it a good time?" she said. She twisted her right hand with her left. "Time's not really ours to judge. Now is it Marjorie?"

"No, Janey, I suppose not. But really, I need to be alone right now."

"No, you don't," she said. "There are things I know that you need to be aware of."

"Can you tell me later, Janey? Tomorrow, maybe? I'm waiting for Benny to return."

"Oh, I'm waiting for so many people to return, Marjorie, that I can't even tell you."

"Well, that's fine then, Janey, because I really can't listen right now."

"Has someone hurt you?" she asked. Her eyes grew wide and she leaned in close so that I could see impatient, blue veins snaking around her temples. "Infected you? Are you infected, Marjorie?" The way her translucent skin pulled taut around her features made her appear vulnerable to injury.

"No, Janey, please. I'm fine. Can you just come back later? Can you do that for me?"

Janey stepped back and took a deep breath. "It's a warm day," she said. "I'll have to walk my dogs slowly."

"Yes," I said, "slow is a good idea."

She turned and stepped off of the porch and walked down the driveway. She stopped at the end of it and said to no one in particular, "Don't block my driveway. There are emergencies and I cannot be blocked in by another vehicle!" She shooed something away from her face and went into her house.

I knew that Benny would soon be home from work and that he would be carrying something. He would either have a new map or a new lamp, I was sure of it. *No more lamps*, I had told him, *not one more stinking lamp*. Some days, Benny just couldn't help himself, and I had a strong feeling that this would be one of those days. Before I was able to shut the door completely, a dull, frenzied bird landed on the porch railing and sang at me desperately before he joined his friends whipping from drab tree to tree. Dusk had fallen and everything had become the same color.

I sat in the living room and looked out the front window. For one lovely moment the street was inactive; but then Janey stormed out of her driveway with her two brilliantly white Alaskan Huskies dragging behind her on blue leashes. They stood out as something too bright to be here. Those dogs always had a look of mild terror in their eyes, although it could have been weariness, or dimness, or confusion. They were so soft and radiant; they broke my heart to look at them. Beauty like that can be hard to take sometimes.

Janey and her dogs walked out of my field of vision and then, not even a minute later, walked back into it. I leaned over the arm of the sofa and watched her hustle them back toward her driveway and into her car—one in the front seat and one in the back—and then she climbed in and gunned the engine and tore out into the street. She was taking one of her drives. I knew them well and looked at my watch and predicted that she would be back in less than five minutes. When the sound of her car became nearly undetectable, the sound of Benny's car replaced it. He was in need of a new muffler; the noise was distressing, although it was nice to have the warning that he would be walking through the door a moment later. He appeared flushed and his hair looked like it had been through a storm. Benny always drove with the windows down. Items surrounded his body.

"Hello, Margie."

"You bought things," I said.

"Bargains," he said. "This fixer-upper table I dove for and these drums were at the Salvy. Beautiful, aren't they?"

"Benny," I said.

"I think they're handmade. They look handmade. I got them for you." He held the drums up for me to take, although I kept my hands by my side. He shrugged and put them on the floor. "And," he said, "because the price was too good to pass up..." He leaned out of the doorway to grab something by its long, thin neck. "I got a black, halogen floor lamp!"

"That's it," I said. "No more, that's it." My stomach clenched and I felt terrifically lonely.

"I promise, Margie," he said, "no more after this one," he paused, "and the silver one in the car."

"The silver one?" I asked.

"It's nice, Margie. I got it for the living room." He kicked the front door shut but because the wood had swelled from the heat, it bounced back open.

"We already have a lamp in the living room," I said. I walked over to the corner where it stood. It was gold and had a heavy base with three light heads that split apart about two feet up and soared out like giant, gaudy, weeping willows. Benny had named it the Woody Allen. I touched the base with my foot and the three light bulbs ignited. It was an ugly sight. "What will we do with Woody?" I asked.

"Oh, Woody stays," he said. "I just thought we could put the halogen in the far corner. The quality of light is fantastic."

"Nobody needs that much light."

"It dims; it brightens. Margie," he said as he turned his hands palm side up, "are you forgetting my seasonal disorder?"

"Quit with the labeling, Benny. You know I hate labels."

"It's scientific, Margie."

"Benny!"

"Alright," he said, "alright. I'll keep it in my office for a while and we'll see. They're just such a bargain, Margie. A whole floor lamp for $19.95. Halogen! What a brilliant invention."

The sound of Janey's car tires spitting gravel out of their way as she drove back into the driveway made us both turn our heads to look out of our front door, which was still open. I moved closer to the door to make sure that both of the dogs were still with her.

"One, two," I counted out loud. Janey used to have three dogs. One went berserk a few months before and jumped out of the car window and into a heavy streak of traffic. I liked to think that in mid air he shut his eyes and slept, never to wake or touch land again.

"Damn," Benny said. "She saw us. You know she's going to come over."

"Benny, I can't do this anymore."

"I know," he said. "Wacko is really driving me nuts. Close the door."

"I mean us, Benny. Don't label her. Her husband is away; she's distressed."

"He's not away," he said. "He's blitzed somewhere. What do you mean, *us*?"

"Us, Benny. You and me. Living here; living together. These ups and downs. These goddamned lamps. The desks. I just can't live like this. Here she comes. Let me talk to her—stay out of it."

"So what about the desks," he said. "Just shut the door. So I have four desks, so what?"

"Five. Keep it down. Don't upset her."

"Five desks, so what? It's my home and I can upset anyone that I want."

"Janey," I said. "Hello. We're a little busy now."

"Busy, busy," she said. "I walked my dogs in the car. It's far too warm for walking on feet." She lifted her toes as if they were breathing.

"I have a lot of maps," Benny said.

"It *is* warm, Janey."

"You can't just fold up those maps," Benny said.

"Benny, please."

"Maps?" Janey asked. "What kind of maps? Who are you working for?"

"None of your business, Janey. Nobody," Benny said.

"Janey why don't you go let your dogs out of the car?" I suggested.

"Don't think it's not the first time I've suspected you of working for the CIA, Mr. Computer man."

"Computer man? Lady, you're nuts! Go down some pills or something."

"Benny, stop! Go upstairs."

"Covert," Janey said. "Top of the line undercover

operations." She leaned in past me and pointed hard at Benny. "I see you on that CIA certified computer, Mr. Computer man." She stepped away from the door and swayed back and forth, wringing her hands. "Don't think I can't see through those sheer curtains. Don't think I don't watch you."

"And don't think that I can't see through yours! Just get the hell out of here, Janey. Crazy Janey." Benny's upper lip tightened and his voice quivered in the way it would when he was over-the-top angry.

"Benny, you're making it worse," I whispered. "Janey, we're friends, right?"

"Can't be too careful," she said. "Can't be too relaxed about matters."

"No, Janey, you can't. How about you go and make a nice dinner for Filbert. You see, I'm trying to talk to Benny about all of that computer stuff."

"Oh," Janey said. "You're trying to get him to get out of the business? I don't want any CIA living next door to me. I've been here a long, long time, you know. I have the right. I have a say in things."

"It's fine, Janey," I said. "I have it all under control. Why don't you go let your dogs inside, OK? Please, Janey?"

She nodded and glowered at Benny before turning and walking towards her car. She calmed down once she opened the doors and the dogs stood beside her. They walked with her into her house as if they weren't quite sure it was where they were supposed to be heading.

I closed the door and turned to Benny. "Why, Benny? Why do you act that way with her? It just makes her worse."

"I'm sick of her, Margie. She's totally nuts! She's schizophrenic. She should be locked up."

"She's *unbalanced*, Benny, that's all. Labels never helped anyone. She was fine last week; she's probably just off her meds. I'll talk to her husband about it."

"Good luck with that. He's a total drunk."

"Do you ever wonder why she makes you so angry, Benny? Did you ever stop to think about that?"

"Because she's annoying," he said. "Because she's probably going to burn our place down one day. What the hell does that mean? Why'd you ask me that?"

"No reason, forget it."

"No, why'd you ask me that?"

"No reason, just forget it."

"You exhaust me."

"You exhaust me."

"You exhaust me more. I'm going to get my lamp from the car." He walked out of the house and slammed the door shut. Again, it bounced back open. He reached his truck and instead of getting the lamp out of the back, he climbed in the driver's side and pulled away. I knew that he would be back shortly once he cooled off. I figured he'd be gone for about fifteen minutes. I closed the door and pushed against it with my hip. The door always swelled with the heat. It was one of those things we had always meant to fix.

While Benny was gone, I played one of the hand-made drums he had brought home. It sounded pretty good, not *plunk plunk*, like I had expected, but more of a *bong, bong.* Benny had a lot of drums. Benny had a lot of most things. When things got hectic for Benny, Benny went collecting. It seemed that things were awfully chaotic inside of Benny, because our home was becoming practically unlivable. I stayed in the living room and played the drum. The living room was my haven. Collections hadn't yet spilled into my living room. "No way that lamp is moving in here," I said out loud. "Goddamned fire hazard is what it is." Bong bong bong. *Not a bad little drum, though*, I thought, *not bad at all.*

I heard noises and peeked out the window. I saw Janey's

husband, Filbert, standing on the sidewalk. He stood drunk and teetering. He yelled toward his house. I opened the front door just enough to hear him.

"Loon," he sang, "looney looney loon! I gotta get a cracker for all the nuts in there." He pointed at his home and laughed. He was good at making himself laugh when he was drunk. I could talk to him when he was sober, but I liked to stay out of his sight when he drank—his eyes became crazed and even though he was an older man, sixty, I thought, he stood firm and square and I didn't want to get him angry. He was vile in many ways, yet he had a fabulous set of strong white teeth. His jaw and his teeth made me shiver, somehow—like they weren't really his, like they were taken from someone much more beautiful. I heard Janey yelling at him about the police and I knew exactly what would happen next. Filbert would rush at her until he stood about three feet from her and he would raise his fist, his finger pointed, and he would say, "You. Are. Crazy," in a quiet, straightforward manner that would make Janey stop talking nonsense and go into the house and make the phone call.

I watched Filbert walk down the street. What a giant of a tragedy. He was handsome once, I gathered, handsome as Janey was lovely. The police drove up just minutes after he left—they were accustomed to this call. They made certain to park down the street so they would not block Janey's driveway. Nobody blocked Janey's driveway. She sat on her front porch in a bathrobe, smoking her cigarette, waiting for them. They smiled as they walked up to her. Hello Janey, I heard them say—so sweet, so calm. I couldn't hear them, but I knew what they talked about: her dogs, the warm evening, the CIA. When she was relaxed they most likely asked her about her medicine. Are you taking it, Janey? Why not? I thought we had an agreement. Maybe you should take it tonight? I watched Janey nod. She was easy now; she would be quiet for the rest of the night. That was just how things went. I closed the door and sat on the floor and played the drum with the eraser ends of two number two pencils.

This wasn't the first time I had decided to leave Benny. It wasn't even the second. A few months before this I was so utterly certain that I was going to leave that I went to the salon and cut my hair off almost entirely. Benny loved my hair long and I had hoped this short cut might make me less appealing to him. Perhaps he'd even ask me to leave.

That evening, after I cut my hair, Benny flew in through the door and headed straight for his office. I heard him shout something about Janey smoking in our driveway, but I didn't care to check things out. Janey could get caught inside her cigarette, burn and float away in a puff for all I cared; I was on a mission. I had made my decision. I had to leave Benny, I told myself, no bones about it.

I poured two glasses of wine and moved slowly toward his office. I'd be calm. I'd remain calm. I'd use reason, say there wasn't enough room left for me in his life. I'd say something like that, I thought, although I hoped it would be even better than that. I hoped it would convey the pain I felt in the soft spot of my throat, like someone jabbed there with their pointer finger over and over and over.

"Benny," I said as I reached his office door. "I brought some wine. Benny?" I shuffled in and peered around a refrigerator box to the place where Benny generally sat when he was in his office. A map stretched out on the desk but his seat sat empty. I noticed, then, the sound of water running in the bathroom. I took the glasses of wine and walked side-step down the hall, holding high the two glasses to keep them from shattering into an old bike frame, a dented file cabinet, a used-to-be wicker chair, a stack of eight-tracks. I stepped into the steam.

"Benny?"

"Hi Marjorie," he said.

Just before the steam covered the glass, I caught my new reflection in the mirror. "I cut my hair," I said. "Hairs. All of them."

He stuck his head out from behind the curtain and looked at me. "Hey," he said, then nothing.

"You don't like it?" I asked.

"Sure," he said, meaning what, I didn't know. "That's the neat thing about hairs," he added. "They grow back."

"I poured wine," I said. "I'll leave it in your office."

As I neared his office, I began to hear those familiar voices outside the window. The voices tore into our home high-pitched and defeated and I knew well that Janey and Filbert were fighting again. I knew well that Janey's blue veins around her eyes pulsed with fear and confusion, and I knew well that Filbert's lips stretched taut, white spittle shaking in the air along with his words. You. Are. Crazy. You. Are. Crazy. You. Are. Crazy.

I wanted desperately to throw open the window and shout down that they were both crazy! *You're. Both. Crazy!* I wanted to shout. *We're. All. Crazy!* I wanted to shout that too. I wanted to tell them that even their damn dogs were crazy, but at least they were beautiful. At least they were that.

I would have, too. I would have shouted all of it—I was that fired up inside. I would have done it, if not for the very, very sad fact that I couldn't cut through Benny's junk and get to the goddamn window.

I drank down one of the glasses of wine. I balanced on one foot, leaned over and placed the other glass on Benny's favorite desk, on one of his Canadian maps; only I caught the stem of the glass on a fold in Ontario and the whole thing tipped over. Bruised red seeped over a good many of the provinces and I couldn't do much to stop it as my feet were caught in a box flap.

I stood like that, trapped, watching the wine tug on the map's fibers, pulling itself across the terrain on its burgundy belly. This is how it will happen, I thought. This is how the conversation will start. Benny will walk in, smelling of hot soap, and he will see the spill and I will tell him that I can't live this way anymore. I will come free of the grip of his collections, and I will float away like a feather.

A door slammed outside. Toothy laughter crept up the brick and into Benny's room. Soon, the cops would saunter up and start to whisper. They would nod. *Are you taking it Janey? Why not? Maybe you should take it tonight.*

"What're you doing, Margie?" Benny placed his lovely hands on my hips as if I were a chair on rollers, a lightweight bongo drum, a lamp, and he gently pushed me away from what caught my leg. He smiled, moved toward his desk as if there were no obstacles whatsoever—just air and other people's confusions. To him it was all very clear. Was it me? I thought. Could I be the clouded one here?

"Damn it, Margie!" He dove forward in an attempt to save his map. "Did you see this? Did you *do* this? Oh, terrific!" He threw his hands up to the heavens. "Of course it's my goddamn Canadian map! You couldn't have spilled on the U.S. could you? I have like, twelve maps of New England alone and look at this, Margie! Look at this! Most of Saskatchewan is utterly incomprehensible now!"

He looked at me, waited for me to explain, apologize, care in the very least about Prince Edward Island flooded by wine. Instead I moved my eyes toward the varicolored light flashes that shot through the window and splattered the far wall—red, blue, white, red, blue, white. The cops were there. Janey was calm now. Janey was growing sleepy and would soon head to bed, a cigarette butt tamped out in the ashtray beside her.

I, too, felt the urge to sleep. I turned away from Benny and felt such exhaustion that I went directly to bed. We'd talk later; I couldn't muster the energy I needed just then. Sleep descended upon me the moment I placed my head down. I woke briefly when Benny crawled in a while later because he whispered into my hair that he liked it short. I fell quickly back into a deep sleep and dreamed of curling up with Janey's dogs, their white fur soft as clouds.

I was still plunking those drums when I heard Benny's car pull up to the house. I looked at my watch—8:30. Maybe we'll just be quiet for the night, I thought. Maybe we'll just pour some wine and watch an old movie. I waited for Benny to come inside. I would be silent when he did. When he wasn't opening the door when I thought he should be, I stood up and looked out of the window. I saw that he was sitting in his truck, with the compartment light on. He sat looking at his hands, which were holding onto the top of the wheel—as if to keep him upright. Perhaps he was thinking. I began to turn away from the window, when I noticed something moving in the grass. A cat, I assumed, but then when I looked again, and let my eyes adjust to the darkness that had fallen, I realized that it was Janey. She sat naked and curled, holding onto her knees and rocking back and forth on our lawn. I went to the door and began to open it and then I stopped. I didn't want to go out there. Why couldn't Janey just leave us alone? I noticed that Benny had climbed outside the truck, then, and was shutting the door— noiseless, double handed, like it could break. He walked around to the front of the truck and while he did, he began to unbutton his plaid shirt. He started at the top and worked his way down to the bottom, which he had to pull out from his jeans. He crept toward Janey and pulled the sleeves off of his arms. All I could hear were the muffled sounds of her crying and the quiet murmurs of Benny's consoling. He placed his shirt over her shoulders and wrapped his arms around her. He pulled her to her feet, which were flat and too long for her gaunt legs. She allowed him to lead her over the lawn and around the bushes between our properties and up her walkway. They turned the corner and I could see her dark tuft of pubic hair, which made her too real, somehow, and I was tempted to look away. I held my gaze, though, and watched as Janey rested her head on Benny's shoulder as he took her inside of her home.

I went to the side windows of the living room and saw the light in her bedroom turn on. I pushed our sheer curtains aside and tried to see though Janey's. I saw no one, only a shadow swoop down on her wall, like something wilting; then there was stillness. I closed my eyes and imagined Benny putting Janey to bed. I pictured him covering her little body with a blanket and speaking so softly to her, so assuredly, that she'd fall asleep while he walked out of her room. He'd flip the porch light on as he left her frenzied home so his path would be well lit. He'd come inside and say he'd like to get rid of some of his collections—three-quarters of everything would be gone in a week—he'd promise me this. We'd have corners again; we'd have rugs. I'd be able to stay.

I opened my eyes as I heard the cry of Janey's screen door open. I jumped back down into the middle of the living room with the drum. Benny opened the door and came in and sat beside me, his shirt buttons askew.

"I just saw the saddest thing," he said.

"Yes," I said.

"I was walking around the park," he said, "where we sometimes feed the geese and I came across a young oak tree."

"How do you know it was young?" I asked.

"It was smaller than the others," he said. "Maybe it was just a small one, a sick one, I don't know. But I saw something around the trunk, at eye level, and I walked closer to get a better look. There were a dozen red roses lined up and taped to the tree—all parallel to one another. Each one two inches apart from the next—all around the tree, attached kind of brutally with clear packing tape. They were like little red-hatted soldiers, tied to a stake. Their heads drooped down—some straight down, some to the side—and their thorns poked through the tape; but they couldn't tear it, they could only make tiny holes. They were trapped. A few petals lay around the base of the tree, as if some attempted to escape but only managed to lose themselves. It was all quite horrible. I can't understand why someone would do that."

He placed the tips of his left-hand fingers to the space between his eyes and I felt the urge to wrap myself around his head, smooth his wind-blown hair; but instead I simply touched his knee with my own.

"Maybe it was supposed to be a gift for someone and they simply went about it all wrong," I said. "Maybe it was wonderful. Maybe it had something to do with love." And then I looked down at the drum he had brought me.

"Well, that's a horrible way to show it," Benny said. "Totally weird and off-base."

He stood and said he was taking a shower. He glided through the jam-packed hallway as if it was empty. He was aware of everything he hoarded and because of this he was able to avoid it, deny it with his twisty walk.

He stopped outside the bathroom and said, "You know Janey's going to burn our house down one day. She'll fall asleep with her cigarette lit and her house will burn and the sparks will fly and catch fire to our own."

He turned into the bathroom, then, and out of his pants pockets fluttered red bits of what I knew were dried petals. He was stuffed with them, I was certain. I'd see them soon inside a sandwich baggie, sealed shut and push-pinned into a corkboard hanging in his office.

I imagined the smell of the smoke of Janey's house burning. It would be black and full of lacquers, paints, the rubber underside of bathmats. I pictured it curling into the sky, swirling around our home, getting sucked inside our opened door. I imagined standing next to Benny, outside of our home, watching the fire, while he shouted to the firemen about Janey still being inside. I would cover my nose with the bottom of my shirt—the smell would be toxic, contagious. I'd want to turn and run but I imagined that Benny would not, and so for whatever reason, I would stay beside him. He'd stand there in the heat of the fire, shouting about Janey—his mouth agape, inhaling fully—as if he knew quite well that all that thickly, crazy smoke already breathed so very deep within him.

you don't *know* me

But I know you. You answered your phone from across the room, yelled, Yes! Hello! It seems I've accidentally kicked my phone across the room but here I come! *Hello, hello!*

It made you nervous that I called. I called you on this knowingness of mine.

But this *you* know: How to obfuscate any action you take at any time. Your hands were simply slick with cocoa butter. You know me, you said. You know how dry my skin can get.

And this *I* know: At the present moment, I am more beautiful than you.

What with?

What with the fact of that dumb mustache, of that false and way-old need to make me laugh. The story of choice? The one of the cops who broke inside your home.

"We had a call of a domestic disturbance, sir."

"But it's just me," you said, "and my two cats."

"What would you have us do?" the officer asked. "We came to the door; we peered into the window; we saw a human head roll over these concrete floors."

You had been returning from work, you told me, and weren't ready for a fight. You said to the officer, "It was probably a cat. More so, I mean, than a human head."

"That, sir, is what we believe now to be true. But what would you have had us do? We felt it important to get inside."

I once felt it important to get inside, too. You seemed to let me get there, but then, alas, and I don't know, something seemed to shut me out.

You don't *know* me. You don't know that I had enjoyed the story of the rolling head—no, running cat—on more than one occasion. You don't know that my favorite part was when you shrugged, leaned back and barrel-chested while you laughed.

But I know you. I know that sometimes you'll say something aloud—How are you? you'll say—and then you'll mouth it silent with your lips. (*How are you?*)

What's happening?

(*What's happening?*)

It was most likely just a cat. More so than a human head.

(*More so than a human head.*)

It seems in this there are two of you—the silent and the talking you. What could you possibly need of me, I wonder. Most likely nothing. You have your cats. You have your few good stories. You have that silent you who reshapes your words and tells them back to you.

Ah, you don't know me, you're probably saying.

(You're probably saying.)

Or possibly not.

(Or possibly not.)

not at all concerned

In the car, at seventy miles an hour, Ronda woke and had a thought.

"I'm worried about the boy."

"He'll be fine," Fred said.

"It could scar him," she said.

"He'll be fine," he said, "he's only four years old, probably won't even notice—like water off a duck's back. Poof! Gone, no problemo."

"We don't know," she said. "It could really upset him."

"In one ear and out the next."

"God, Fred. How can you be so flip?"

"He'll be fine, Ronda. No permanent damage, I guarantee. Right, son? How ya doing back there, tiger?"

"Not tiger, Daddy, Smokey the *Girl* Cat."

"Oh, right, my fault."

"You excited to see Grandma and Grandpa, Honey?" Ronda asked her son.

"I'm a cat on a roof," the boy said.

"Honey? I asked you a question."

"Son, why you got to be a girl cat? Why Smokey the *Girl* Cat?"

"I'm a cat on the roof of the car," the boy said.

"Sweetie, I asked you if you are excited to see your Grandma and Grandpa?"

"He nodded, Ronda, let him be," said Fred.

"What do you mean he nodded?"

"I mean he nodded. I saw him nod, yes, in the rearview. Leave him be, he's in character."

"Well," she said, "*I* didn't see it."

"Cause you got that stiff neck," Fred said. "You can't even turn around, your neck's so stiff."

"That sounds accusatory," Ronda said.

"Nope, nope," Fred said, pointing to the sky. "Not accusatory, factual. It is *factual* and my stating it does not make it *accusatory*."

"Well," she said, "it felt like you were finger wagging."

"No finger wagging," he said. "Look, we're almost there. See the trees? They're all getting shorter."

"And sharper," Ronda said. "Trees out here are mean, huh?"

"Less green," Fred said. "A bit grayer, I believe."

"I asked you if you thought they were meaner out here," Ronda said.

"Defensive," Fred said. "I'm going to have to go with defensive over mean. How you doing back there son? You OK?"

"Yes," the boy said, "and you know what?" He leaned forward so that his face was between his parents' shoulders. "I am not at all concerned that there aren't any giraffes out here." He laughed and fell back into his seat. "I'm not concerned at all!"

When the boy fell asleep, Ronda gripped her thighs with her long fingers and asked, "Who splits up in their sixties? Who does that? It's not normal, I tell you. It's not. They have a grandchild to consider, for God's sake."

"For *everybody's* sake," Fred said.

"Yes," she said, "Yes, you're right! For *everybody's* sake." Then she wrinkled her brow and looked at Fred.

"Don't amuse me, Fred," she said. "Do me that one, small favor."

* * *

Once they reached Ronda's parents' street, Fred was instructed to drive around the block while Ronda explained some things to her son regarding her parents' recent separation.

"Baby? Honey? Wake up, kitty cat, we're at your grandma's house."

"I'm basking in the sun," the boy said. "I'm a calico cat and I am basking in a sun beam."

"That's nice, honey," Ronda said. "Will you listen to me for a minute? I need to talk to you about your grandparents."

"Come on, Ronda," Fred said. "I don't want to drive around the block again."

"Patience is a virtue, dear."

"Just try to speed it up."

"OK, sweetie, are you listening? I just want you to know that your Grandma and Grandpa have moved some furniture around. They moved it around quite a lot."

"Smokey the Girl Cat is not allowed on the furniture," the boy said. "You know why?"

"In fact, honey," she continued, "they moved it around so much, that all of Grandpa's things are out in the carport."

"Because Smokey the Girl Cat has fur and will shed all over things," he said.

"Isn't that a hoot, honey? All of Grandpa's furniture is outside under the carport. And you know what, honey?"

"What?" he asked. Ronda paused for a minute, surprised that he was paying her some attention.

"Well," she said, "your grandpa liked his stuff out in the carport so much, that he decided to move out there! Isn't that a scream?"

The boy held his stomach and laughed and laughed and Fred pulled the car up in front of the house.

"Water," Fred said, "off a duck's back. Simple as that."

Ronda looked straight ahead as Fred brought the car to a stop, not wishing to look at her father's new home just yet.

"This is so terribly humiliating," she said. "The entire neighborhood can see him out there. I can't believe I was made by these people."

"I don't think so," Fred said, and then he looked at Ronda, who was pinching her lips together so that they wrinkled like the top of a pear. "I mean I don't think it's humiliating," he said. "I am very surprised that you were made by them. Honest, I am."

Ronda knew better then to place her mother second—under any circumstance—and so she shuffled her husband and son through the front door, with just a quick wave to her father. They were there for a good ten minutes before Ronda told her mother that they were going outside to visit with *him*.

"No mention of his name in here," her mother said. "Do you hear me? Monsieur and I get along nicely without mentioning that man's name in here. Don't we Monsieur?"

Monsieur, her mother's high strung parrot, bobbed his head up and down and said, "Monsieur, Monsieur is sweet. *Je suis chocolat! Je suis mais sucre!*"

"I hate that bird," Ronda said.

Her mother spun around with a wooden spoon dripping red sauce onto the floor. She held it up, not in a threatening manner, but as if it were her microphone—the way in which she communicated. "Apologize, Ronda. No cheap bird shots allowed. Do you hear me? This is *my* house now."

"Pardon me, Monsieur," Ronda said. "We'll be visiting the strange man in the carport, now."

"You know what, Grandma?" the boy said on his way outside. "Smokey the Girl Cat and Monsieur are friends. It's an anomaly."

"That's nice, sweetie," his grandma said. "All well and good."

Once they walked through the laundry and out the side door, Fred began to laugh at the home his Father-in-law had created under the carport.

"Good god, Pops," he said. "This is great!"

"Don't you laugh at this," Ronda said. "Don't you two start with the jokes. This is not funny."

"Oh but Ronda," Fred said, "it *is* funny. He's made a, what is this Pops, a changing room? He has made a changing room out of a shower curtain and rod."

"I always said," Ronda's father began, "that a man's greatest wealth is found in his resourcefulness."

Ronda and Fred walked around the carport, while her father explained what everything was.

"Over here is my bedroom," he began. "It's quite nice, waking with the cool breeze on my face every morning. Even the hottest Texas morning holds a little bit of cool; I don't suppose you knew that? And over here is my living room—I spend a lot of time here. The woman inside is kind enough to allow me to extension out some electricity so that I can power my TV and my lamps and such."

"*The woman inside?*" Ronda said. She jutted her neck forward, pulled her shoulders back. When she realized she was doing so she shook it out and checked her posture—if Fred caught her straining he'd coo like a pigeon. This she knew from experience.

"And over here is my office." He pointed to a small, kid's sized desk and chair. "Imperative."

"Grandpa," the boy said. "Do the crow birds come inside and pester you?"

"Daddy," Rhonda said, "the neighbors can see everything that you do; you have no walls, no privacy!"

"No need for any," her father said. "It's a little like camping. I just wave at the neighbors and they go and wave back. How y'all doing, I say, Fine, fine, and that's that. It really is starting to feel like home. Do you agree?"

"No," said Ronda.

"To each his own," said Fred.

"Most definitely," said the boy.

* * *

Ronda's mother slammed things around in the kitchen and Ronda figured that it was time to eat and so she led Fred and the boy inside.

"Goodbye, Daddy," she said.

"Well," he said. "Not a one of you will be eating with me? I have a dining room set folded up somewheres out here."

Ronda took a deep breath and smelled her mother's fabulous red sauce. Fred's mouth began to water so fast, it almost stung. They felt relieved when the boy said that he wanted to eat out with Grandpa.

"All right, honey," Ronda said to the boy. "You may eat out here. Do you have a refrigerator too, Daddy?"

"Of course," he said, "but that is just for my soda pop. The woman inside is kind enough to send my meals out through this little breakfast nook which I cut myself with a jig saw."

"Fabulous."

Ronda went inside and her mother handed her a plate of lasagna.

"I'll need two, Ma. My kid wants to eat with his Grandpa."

"Grandma's not good enough for him I see."

"Guess not," Ronda said. "Now, how come you keep feeding him, Ma? I mean if you can't stand to live with him, why are you feeding him?"

"It's all part of the bargain," her mother said. "He continues to take care of the bills, and I continue to take care of the food. It's all very fair." She placed a piece of lasagna on a plate for the boy—far more than a child that size could eat.

"That's too much," Ronda said. "He'll never eat that much."

"The man outside will finish it, then. You know he's always been a scavenger."

Ronda delivered the plates, "Through the breakfast nook!" as her mother insisted and then sat down at the dining room table with her mother and Fred, who were discussing the reasons for the separation.

"It was everything, Fred. Everything! He was always under foot. His deviated septum, his breathing, everything! He can be like a child, sometimes, with his inventions. Did he tell you about his latest? He bought one of those "You Invent It" kits for far too much money and he spends all of his time filling in those damn graph paper squares when it will all amount to nothing! I just kept telling him, *It will amount to nothing!* Do you understand? And he would get angry and it was a terribly destructive cycle. This is all for the best."

"What sort of inventions, Ma?"

"Oh, soda can thimble was the first one. You know, to protect the finger when you open a can. Belt buckle slash travel shaving kit, was another. He was certain that one would sell. Let's see, Oh, yes! And that blasted Port a Potty for the long road trip fiasco. That was just disgusting. I told him, *Pop that is just disgusting.* Lord knows what he's thinking up out there, now. His wheels keep spinning out there in that carport." She started to laugh. "Get it? Wheels spinning in the carport?" She continued to laugh until she started to cry, just a little. Just enough to make Fred look away and Ronda feel like maybe there was some hope for her whacked-out family after all.

"He just needs to feel important, Ma. Like he's doing something worthwhile. It's hard to be retired."

"Don't tell me," her mother said. "Don't tell me how hard it is to be retired!"

"But Ma," Fred said. "You didn't work."

"I worked!" she said. "I most certainly did work! For five years I worked! I was a secretary and a damn good one!"

"That's right," Fred said. "You worked for Pop."

"I ran that lousy office," she said. "That man was a mess until I came in and set up some systems. He should have been the one to leave and care for the kids, you know. I would have made that company grow like a weed. I should have known he was a basket case when I went for that interview."

"What happened at the interview, Ma? You never told me about it." Ronda said.

"No I did not. I didn't want you to think that your father was a fool. No child should think that. But now, I suppose since we're separated, I can tell you." She put her fork down and placed her hands in her lap. "I was well into the interview, telling him about my schooling, when he tilted his head back and looked up at the ceiling. I, of course, looked at the ceiling as well, and there was nothing there, so I looked back at him and he told me that he had gone to the coast that past weekend and that the sand and the stink of oil sometimes bothered his nose. I wasn't sure where he was heading with the story, so I didn't comment. But then, he proceeded to get out of his chair and pull his handkerchief to his face and then he moved right next to where I was sitting. Well, I became nervous when he started to lie down beside me until he said, 'Sometimes I get nosebleeds.' So there he was, lying on the floor beside me, bleeding." She laughed. "The strangest part was that he asked me to continue with my interview. All polite but honest about the vulnerability of the body, 'Forgive me,' and 'Sell yourself,' he said." She sighed. "I recall that I giggled and flipped my hand—just enough to let him know that I did not judge his imperfections—and then I sold myself as if he sat across from me, as dignified as any man can be."

"That's a sweet, disturbing story you tell, Ma," Fred said. "Leaning more towards the disturbing."

"Leaning more towards the sweet, you mean." Ronda said.

"*Un bon bon!*" the parrot squawked.

They were silent for a minute and they began to eat their lasagna, when they heard a scuffle outside.

"What was that?" Ronda said as she moved over to the window.

"It sounded like a tussle," Fred said.

"It sounded worse than that," said Ronda's mother. "It sounded like a full-out altercation, a fighting of wills!"

The door to the carport opened, then, and Ronda could see her father gently shove the boy into the house.

"Oh my god, sweetie!" Ronda shouted. "What happened?"

The boy walked over to her with a smile on his face and blood dripping down his cheek from his forehead. Ronda's mother ran into the kitchen and grabbed a damp cloth.

"Son, are you all right? Tell us what happened!" Fred was looking into the boy's eyes to see if there was any sign of delirium.

"I'm OK, Daddy," the boy said.

His grandfather hollered through the breakfast nook, "Just a minor scuffle. Everything is OK now."

"Pop," Fred yelled, "What happened?"

"Well," he answered. "It seems that Smokey the Girl Cat happened upon a little baby grackle bird hopping in the grass."

"Smokey the Girl Cat doesn't like birds," the boy said. "But she kind of likes the babies."

"So any which way," his Grandpa continued. "Girl Cat and I were just watching the bird hobbling around when we thought maybe we could assist the little fella back into the tree. You know, give him a little boost."

"Daddy!" Ronda yelled. "Don't you know never to touch a baby bird?"

"Well," he said, "I suppose that just might be the lesson to be learned here."

"We didn't touch it," the boy said. "We only reached for it when the grackle birds got mad. They were incensed, Mommy. They started clucking and then they dove straight for my head and pecked at it."

"*J'accuse!*" screeched the parrot, all aflutter.

"Son," Fred said, "you worry me sometimes."

"I'm not at all concerned," the boy said. "Smokey gets in and out of trouble all the time." He started to laugh and Ronda hugged him.

Ronda's mother stood in the kitchen and looked at the sink. "Fred, ask the man outside if he was pecked at by those birds as well."

"Pop!" Fred yelled. "They get you, too?"

"Well," he answered. "I suppose they got to me a bit, yes."

"Fred," Ronda's mother continued. "Ask him if they got him on his bald spot."

"Pop!" Fred yelled. "On your bald spot?"

"Yes," he answered. "I suppose that's where they got me."

"Fred," Ronda's mother said, "ask him if he is bleeding from that spot."

"You bleeding Pop?" Fred yelled.

"Well," he answered. "I suppose I am. But just a little bit. It certainly isn't a gusher."

Ronda's mother continued to stare into the sink. "Never know what is going to turn into a gusher," she said, louder than she had been speaking before. "Sometimes something starts off as a trickle and then it goes and turns into a gusher. Sometimes things get carried away on themselves and start to pour like rain. Sometimes something little gets going and then it grows and grows and turns into a geyser—shooting out like there's no tomorrow! Spouting out like there is no other choice but to be what it has gotten itself all worked up to be: a wet, gushing, streaming bleed with no chance in the world of stopping it!" She turned around and Fred and Ronda and her grandson were all staring at her. "Am I making sense?" she shouted. "Am I speaking sanely? Does everybody know what the heck I'm talking about?"

All three of them nodded. Ronda's father yelled through the breakfast nook. "I know full-out what you mean, Mother. You are speaking clear as a birdbath. I understand exactly whereof you speak."

Ronda's mother stuck her head around the kitchen doorway so she could see her husband's face through the nook. "Well then, Pop," she said softly, "I believe that you

should bring yourself inside so that I can fix you up right."
And he smiled, shut the opening to the nook, and made his
way toward the door that would lead him back into his home
for the first time in a long time.

dog park

We met an old friend and his old dog. We went off leash on the lush Buffalo grass. He and I—this old friend, I mean—talked mostly of divorce, something we shared between us.

"Is someone in my back yard every night?" I asked.

"I don't think so," he said, "but it's hard to say."

"The dog, she's always jumping up and looking out there. It could simply be rats, but still, it frightens me."

"I have a side alley," he said, "as you well know. My dog goes bananas on it every night around eight." He called to his dog then—she had run too far—and as she came back to us, he said, "Sometimes seven o'clock in the winter."

Our dogs are of different ages and one tired before the other.

"Let's get them some water," my old friend said, "and avoid these children on the way."

I agreed. We re-leashed them and veered away from the kids. One was having a tantrum.

"Dogs don't like tantrums," he said. "It unnerves them."

I nodded, but thought he spoke mostly of himself. Men don't like tantrums, I thought. Something is happening in the world.

"When you lived here," he said, "when you were married— when we were both married—I thought you were so beautiful."

"I'm still beautiful," I said. I pressed the metal button so the dog could drink from the dog-height water fountain.

"Ma'am," my old friend said in falsetto. "That's not for dogs. That's for very, very, very tiny people." He placed his hand on my back and breathed out a laugh. "More beautiful," he said. "You have nostalgia on your side now."

We embraced and then we parted, both with our leashed dogs. After a run in the park, mine tends to curl herself like a donut and fall into a deep sleep. Sometimes when I look at her, I feel this sleep will last a lifetime, but then, at some point, I trust she will wake.

lumbering beasts

A nna should not have worn that shirt that night. You're so stupid, Anna, to have worn that stupid, stupid shirt that night. The fact of it changed her, hardened her in a way she never knew she could be hardened.

She walked into her bathroom, marveled at the cleanliness—a level of clean that her recently ex-husband had no comprehension of whatsoever (the man, after all, loved the bruised parts of apples more so than the fresh); a level of clean that could only be found in a tacky new condo that perched atop a Starbucks Café. When she moved out of their house she sought safety and spic-and-span. Keeping Austin Weird was not her concern.

It was a cute shirt—the color, at least, and the shape—but damn, that little deer silhouette really fucked her over. What she should have done was this: the moment she felt him—the one she'll now refer to as *The Man*—look at her one blink too long to be anything but direct, she should have excused herself from the table, claimed the beer made her have to pee, go into the washroom and turn her tee shirt inside out. She should have felt The Man's intentions and she should have thought: *I have to hide this image of the deer.* Stupid, stupid. With her it was always hindsight. She should learn to walk backwards into rooms, hold a mirror out in front of her to see behind, to know then how to respond to situations immediately, and with some level of success.

However, Anna did not do this that night; she did not hide the deer. She simply sat there, stunned by The Man's stare. The bar was dark, but of course she managed to sit directly where the light that occasionally shot out of the bathroom door struck. *Kapow!* The light blasted her eyes, made the little deer silhouette on her shirt stop and tremble. The man noticed this, she knew. He took it all in. At one point she felt The Man had decided something about her, something that made her heart *thump thump* fast inside her chest. *I'm no longer married,* his decision made her remember. *My husband left me for the coffee girl at Jo's and I'm no longer married.*

The Man came and sat beside her. They exchanged very few words. She noticed that he smelled vaguely of the tone of sepia. His forearms traveled down quite nicely toward his hands. At that moment, she felt glad that she had worn that shirt that night, because it showed off her clavicles when she pulled her shoulders down just so. It showed the contours of her breasts when she breathed in deeply, when she swallowed in the entire, thrilling early summer night.

She went home alone that night, but she had told him of her and she knew well that he would be in touch. She knew well that he had practiced this technique before—these pauses, these pregnant gaps in time.

"I'm writing to you," The Man finally emailed a few days later, "because I'd like for you to teach me how to swim."

"I'm writing back," she replied, "because my corporate-style complex has a good-sized pool. Please do not be put off by the large Texas star on the front gate. I'm truly a bohemian."

In his swimsuit he was surprisingly good-looking. Surprising because his was the sort of handsome that, if caught in a still photo, might appear mildly bread-loafish; although the way he moved within it, the way he spoke and side-smiled and kept his eyes steady like he did, gave him a star-like quality. That tattoo, as well—a crouching tiger on the inside of his forearm—lent something to his panache. Again, Anna felt that thumping heart thing. She pulled her shirt up over her head, revealing her new pink bikini that may or may not— she suddenly realized—become transparent when wet.

He swam like a hippo, an animal that is technically strong and efficient, but aesthetically displeasing. Anna wanted him to stop. She wanted to watch him walk again around the bean-shaped perimeter of the pool so she'd re-experience that intense fluttering inside her middle. She stood then, in the shallow end and said she felt a little water-logged, and she looked away as he floated his largeness over to her. She thought of her nearly ex-husband for a moment, of how his lanky limbs became so graceful in the water, became so graceful when he'd hold onto his acoustic guitar and roll his twiggy fingers over the strings. Wild sadness came in waves to her those days. But then she felt a thickened, unfamiliar finger touch her belly.

"You once had a piercing here," he said.

She nodded, said that that was in her twenties when it had seemed cute, but now it felt too obvious so she took it out. She felt her insides flip about as his finger plugged the dotted scar. This was the first time The Man had touched her and it was a promising touch, to say the least.

"I'm not free to have a long relationship," he rumbled.

"I'm not looking to have one," she breathed back to him.

And here the deal was made.

Looking back she knows the deal was less a deal, less an *agreement*, than it was an arrangement that The Man created, an arrangement in which Anna agreed to be a participant. What else was expected of her at the time? To be wanted was to be wanted and when one was as *unwanted* as Anna was by her own husband, then to be hunted seemed exciting and almost kind. *To be hunted* was a sort of *to be wanted* and whatever, she was game for whatever. Again, his touch had been promising and hell, they were both adults.

It would last a week only, this arrangement. As he had said he was not free for anything long term and Anna knew damn right well that on Friday his girlfriend would return from wherever she had been, and that on Saturday The Man and his girl would start shopping for apartments. They'd look first up north, which surprised Anna as she thought The Man was more of an urban cowboy; he seemed to be the sort of man who needed sidewalks and coffee shops on every corner, but then again, Anna did not seem to be the sort to live behind a gate on which a large Texas star threatened all who dared to enter. It made her think of snakes. It made her think of cowboys with boots to protect them from the snakes. The Man had been unfazed by the star, he said, by the way. Bravado rarely bothered him. Meekness, now that could really make a man angry. He meowed like a kitten and for a moment Anna felt frightened to have him in her bed. Who are you? she thought. Where is the man I've been sleeping next to all of these years? He was a different man; he was a vastly different species of man. He would never, for instance, say *yeah yeah yeah* over and over again like a parrot when he found an intimate moment to be pleasurable.

In the morning she said she was going out for coffee and he said that was fine. He said he'd also like one of those scone-things. Where was she going, anyway? he asked. Downstairs to the Starbucks?

Jo's, she said, although it was a few blocks down on Congress.

Oh, he said. I like Jo's coffee.

Yes, she agreed with him there. Jo's served excellent coffee.

She took her time walking because it was hot. She meandered around the neighborhood and then she paused on the corner.

She feared for a moment that her ex might be there and if so then what? If so then nothing, she concluded; she'd just look at him and see someone she once knew who no longer cared to know her.

He wasn't there, although *she* was. Anna had seen her a few times before, always at a distance, while the girl sat outside the coffee shop smoking a cigarette. Who smokes cigarettes anymore anyway? What an indication of weakness, she thought. Meekness, she thought then. *Meow, meow, meow.* The world was full of kittens.

She walked directly to the counter. She wanted no one else to serve her but this girl.

Two large coffees, she ordered. One chocolate scone.

Leave room for milk? the coffee girl asked.

Leave room for milk, she said.

Anna watched her pour the coffee, tap the keys on the register. Woof, she thought. Not pretty. Not pretty like she was pretty, which was a natural, gentle sort of pretty. OK so maybe this girl had some pretty in her, but it felt blue and unsure to Anna. He left me for this? She would have preferred a great beauty, a step up; at least then she could admire his drive. Now she just felt embarrassed to have once known a man who would make such a bad decision. Of course she was being unfair—she knew well that beauty does not always immediately radiate. She watched the girl wrap the scone in wax paper. She thought maybe she'd see kindness or grace or something more elusive than beauty in the way that she used her hands. She didn't, though. Instead she saw clumsiness. She thought of the man in her bed and realized that clumsiness abounds. Large, lumbering beasts roamed freely in this city. Still, the thought of The Man in her bed shot hot excitement through her body. She watched the coffee girl slide the scone into the brown paper bag, though, and felt a distracting punch of nausea hit the back of her throat.

Cash or charge? the coffee girl asked.

Oh, Anna said. Charge.

She watched the girl's face as she handed her the card. The girl flinched and reddened when she read her name. She knows my name, Anna thought. She is shaking inside. She wants to crumple into a ball on the floor of the coffee shop. She kept her eyes averted—the coffee girl did—busied her hands with the sugar packets as she waited for the card to be approved.

Thank you, Anna said, after she signed the receipt.

The girl looked up, her eyes *why*-ing desperately at her until Anna turned away.

Why *now*? Anna thought. How about: why hadn't I *before*? How about: why don't I *again*? She looked down and counted the sugar packets in her tray: 12. Enough to sweeten the whole complex pool.

When she reached her building, she paused by the star on the gate and closed her eyes. She imagined the coffee girl's face. She imagined holding her face in her hands and bringing her lips to her own. She imagined the smell of her, the taste of her tongue. Cigarettes, she thought. Coffee. She imagined looking into the eyes of this girl and feeling something desperate pull her in—something from within that was too difficult to deny. It was so *impossible* to deny, in fact, that she'd have to make the decision to stop knowing someone who she had known for so many years in order to start knowing this other. I don't see it, Anna thought. I just don't. The girl's hands had moved like dog paws—*slappa slappa pound thud.* Anna keyed her condo number into the gate pad and swore her own hands could be two fluttered birds. She whistled as she climbed the stairs.

The Man sat on her sofa, reading a book she recognized as one of hers that had previously sat undisturbed on her coffee table. She wanted him to put it down and to quit looking so at ease in her condo. He remained very comfortable—comfortable enough to not thank her for the coffee. She couldn't watch him eat the scone. He dipped it deeply into his cup and ate half in one bite and when Anna saw this she looked away. When he was finished eating he looked at her and said she looked hot.

I'm not hot, she said, but then she understood. They moved into the bedroom and she spent the rest of the morning feeling lanky and twisted, embarrassed when the sun shot through the window, threatening her with that god-awful chance that heaven truly existed and that it was looking down at her now, as she performed these foul, animalistic acts.

Two more days remained of the arrangement and Anna was spent and irritated, but addicted, now, to the gross physicality of The Man. She should never have opened her home to another body—she'd feel its absence when it left—this she was sure of. She could hardly look at The Man, hardly talk to him, so they remained tangled, mostly, in heaving knots of distraction in various parts of her home. After one such entanglement she again craved coffee and declared she was heading to Jo's to get some.

Scone? she asked.

Muffin, he said.

As she turned and walked out of her condo, her back facing the man, she felt the urge—and didn't fight it—to mouth the word, *foreskin,* as if she was admitting the fact of it to herself for the very first time. I've lived in a bubble, she thought. I've lived in a world where all men cut them off. All men, of course, meant her husband; because for a time—a very long time—he was.

The coffee girl sat smoking on a car stop in the parking lot. She saw Anna, stood, stomped her cigarette with her flip-flopped foot and went inside, but not to the register. Anna looked for her to emerge from the back and waved away the other barista's offer to take her order. I want the other girl, she mouthed.

Excuse me?

The other girl, she said. I want her.

What?

Anna sighed, moved toward the register. Never mind, she said. Two coffees, one muffin.

Leave room for milk?

Sure, Anna said.

One of those waves came over her. It hit her hard this time and so she leaned forward and held onto the counter. Who was this man in her condo? she thought. She brought her hands to her face and the scent sickened her—the unfamiliarity of that scent was too much to take and she nearly fainted.

Are you alright? the barista asked.

Anna steadied herself and smiled. Yes, she said, I'm fine. And then she took her tray toward the back of the café. She placed the tray down on a table and kept moving forward, kept moving through that door marked for employees only. She was on the other side of the door before she noticed that she had actually pressed her fluttered bird-hand upon it and shoved.

The clumsy girl, the coffee girl, sat with her back toward her, her face toward her computer.

She's checking her email, Anna thought. She's looking for a message from him.

Did he write? Anna asked.

Who? the girl asked back, and then she turned and then she jumped and said, Oh.

That's OK, Anna said. It's none of my business because I don't know him anymore.

The girl said nothing, but she leaned against the computer table, which moved and so she stumbled.

There's a man in my condo, Anna said. I know him through someone, and we have this arrangement that is about to end, but I needed to see you to get the guts up to go back to him for the final day or so.

Why did you need to see me? the coffee girl asked.

Please get lovely, Anna thought. Please impress upon me something, anything at all. I'm not angry, Anna said, so please, relax. Sit down.

The girl sat and so too did Anna. You have beautiful ankles, Anna said, because she did. The coffee girl's ankles were thin and brittle, gazelle-like. Her toes, too, filthy in her flip flops, were brown and elegant.

There's a man in my condo, Anna said again. The thought of him excites me. Is it that way for you?

Is what? the coffee girl said, clumsily, spastically flipping her hair.

Tell me, Anna said.

The girl tugged at her bra, underneath her right breast. Jesus, she said.

We're just talking, Anna said. You know something I used to know and we're just talking, don't you see? There's a man in my apartment and I'm just asking you a simple question and I'd think you'd think, well, at least she deserves an answer to that simple question—

OK fine! the coffee girl said. Yes. Fine. Yes. A little.

The thought of him?

Yes.

It's exciting? Anna asked.

Yes.

Your insides jump?

Jesus, the coffee girl said.

Do they?

Yes, she said. They jump.

Do you ever look at him and wonder who he is? Anna asked. Do you ever wonder why he's in your bed?

OK, the coffee girl said, and stood. That's enough.

But it's not, Anna said. It's really, oh so not enough.

The coffee girl held the door open for Anna and Anna paused by her extended arm, tried to smell the aroma of her pit, the flavor of her hair. I smell him on you, she said, but realized that it sounded accusatory, when really she meant that for a moment, when she smelled him, she thought perhaps she could move inside this girl and call her home.

OK so The Man was not circumcised. This was a decision his mother had made. Anna felt overwhelmed while in the presence of such a decision and often shut her eyes to it; but when she did she only imagined it and when she imagined it, she became excited. Only hours remained before the arrangement ended, and Anna felt the need to fill her place with bodies—stuff the sofa with thighs, the kitchen cupboards with shoulders, the bathtub with knees. She wanted to rub the man's scent upon her carpet, her off-white painted walls. Dig your toenails into the carpet, she implored him. Rub the back of your head into my pillows. Piss in my toilet. Spit in my sink.

Where has she been? Anna asked, as he laced his shoes to go.

It's just been a week, The Man said. It hasn't been all that long.

And she just waited? she said.

She's away, he said. Are you going for coffee?

You should stop with the muffins, Anna said. The scones, too.

I'm heavier; I'm twice the man, The Man started to say.

A different species, she added. One I don't know.

Where's my bag? he asked.

I'll get it, she said. She went into the bedroom, shoved his white shirts back inside. Just a minute! she called, as she moved into the bathroom to grab her own shirt from the hamper. She turned it inside out so the deer silhouette wasn't immediately apparent. She brought it into the bedroom and shoved it inside his bag.

Are you coming? he asked.

I'm zipping it, she said. And then she did.

He left and her place filled with silence. Anna went into

the bathroom to put on her bikini. She looked light, as if she hadn't been eating for days and days. In the kitchen she stuffed her mouth with bread and fatty cheese. She walked out of her front door and hopped down her stairs. She began to think of The Man, of his clumsiness, the lovely way he fell into her over and over, but she wouldn't allow that and instead thought of the clumsiness of the coffee girl at Jo's. She'd go visit her later, she thought. She'd skulk in the back corner and watch her fumble with the sugar packets, watch her spill the frothing milk over onto the saucer. She'd wait until the girl was alone, until she was feeling frightened and deserted, as everyone eventually feels—and then she'd approach. Lumbering beasts, she thought. Everywhere, everywhere. Predator and prey. She was no longer the latter. She caught sight of the large Texas star on her gate. *Hiss*— she made the sound with her tongue, into the air. *Hiss, hiss, hiss, all you meowing kittens. Roar, roar, roar, all you scrambling deer.*

come to me at night

They come to me at night. I have to cash my check; I see their bodies next to yours; I see the rent is due; I see you holding them inside your arms.

I'm out of stamps. I think of how you wanted me at every moment when we met—outside a tom cat screams into the window—as I wanted you; I hate to think you wanted them, their skinny bodies, whatever minds. I smell the spray; my roommate died but before she did she said the cats would come; I know you keep in touch with them; I wonder what they say to you and how you speak to them of me.

I can't forget to pay the gas bill. Do they talk to you as if they know something more of you than *me?* I know something but not everything not nothing from those years you hardly talk about; that smell will stain my place and then more cats will come; I know you burned yourself; I know you brought to bed a lot of girls; I know I should to be concerned about the scars but they don't come to me at night.

My roommate died on the West End Highway; it was awful and she keeps getting bills sent from the hospital although she's dead. The ones you say were toxic I assume you mean *real sexual* and then they come to me at night; I see their sweated bodies wrapped with yours.

I have an appointment set for the day after next; you said you thought you might be firing blanks and then I feel a

kick into my chest—two kicks, three, seven at least—my cat
is going crazy at the stinky tom outside the window and the
birds are waking, screaming: *I'm not dead!* You say you want
my babies but well, just *no,* not now, just *no* not yet.

They come to me at night; I'm more beautiful I know
you love me; my roommate's family threw her things out in
the trash and left me with her furniture I didn't want; you
helped me deal with all of that; I need some envelopes as
well; I'll get them when I get the stamps; you are a Nine One
One Man for all the planet, for all the women you once held
in bed and said those things you say to me only this I *know*—
only this I *think* I know—that we will last.

The birds make sleep prohibitive; the tom cat stink sits on
my tongue; in just two days I'll start to bleed; I know you love
me; there's no comparing still they come to me at night, at
nights like this that turn to mornings when I turn to you and
curse the birds—*I curse the birds!*—the ones who made it
through this night; they made it through this God-long night.

at shabu shabu

Thomas ordered two plates of quail eggs. He knew the term for bird-vagina, and this made Hillary think of his ex-girlfriend who rubberized dead ones she found in the street. Not vaginas, of course, but birds. She rubberized these and placed them under glass. Beautiful things, moist with death.

Thomas and Hillary had grown close in their year together, as in: He passed gas freely when in her presence. He implied that he preferred she did not. She would show decorum, she said, once he showed some chivalry. She implied this meant he pay for Shabu-Shabu, so Thomas acquiesced, and said, *Let 'er rip!*

At Shabu-Shabu they cooked their own concoction within their own bins of boiled water. At nineteen it all roared up; at thirty-two it all went still; there was logic there, only they didn't get it. The cabbage cooled the water, then they simply spun the dial.

Hillary watched his hand plunk in small eggs. Such lovely, scuffed-up, wide-palmed paws. And such darling, little eggs! She wondered how the quail felt giving up such perfect things. Everything is perfect, she supposed, if never given the chance to prove itself to be anything but that.

Thomas turned to her and smiled. He loved to Shabu-Shabu, and she loved to see him happy. She smiled back but suddenly felt sorry for the eggs and turned away. She focused on her water. It's hard to get it right. Sometimes the vermicellli went in too early and coagulated to make the water less like water, more like phlegm. This was when the Shabu waitress walked on over, full of pity, and poured more water in the bin. And by, *in the*, she meant, *in hers*. It happened every time. It was hard to get it right.

It wasn't so much the eggs, she thought, but more the stunted potential of them. Their mystery was gone; they'd soon be covered in spicy Taiwanese barbeque sauce, and slurped into Thomas' mouth. She looked at him and found him once again to be beautiful to her. There are worse places, she supposed, and then she kissed him there, on his mouth, where the eggs would soon be fated.

A stoner sat a table away, with knotty hair and plates so piled with potential eating it could almost cause some envy, and told a story to his stoner friend about the time he went to China and how the shrimp come to the table live.

"And when I say *live*," he said, "I mean, as in, still *fighting*."

Hillary didn't have to strain to listen; his high had made his voice grow loud.

"I tossed one in the water," he said, "and get this man, it jumped right out! It wiggled off the table and started heading for the door. And I was like this": He curled his hand into a fist and raised it shoulder-height. "*Go for the gold, little buddy!*"

Hillary pictured this shrimp running for freedom and thought she too would cheer it on. She'd also, most likely, lift her feet from the ground to make sure it didn't skitter over her toes on the way.

The man's friend stared at him, took his attention away from his own boiling pot and dropped a dumpling in so that it caused a splash that hit his arm. He felt the spot, then leaned back and said: "Ouch. There is potential for some pain in here." Just a few moments later it seemed he forgot he had said anything at all because he gestured to the steam and said, "There is potential to suffer harm."

It's true, Hillary thought. There is always potential to

suffer harm unless all potential is stunted. By now she was obsessed with Thomas' two plates of quail eggs. He pulled her chair over so she sat closer to him then. He kissed her head and she felt better. Still, she thought, *two* plates of eggs? Two plates of such delicate things.

Cloaca—that's what it's called. It's vaginal, but only in so much as it's an opening. Most male birds have the very same thing and it only takes a moment or two to pass all of the important stuff through from bird to bird. *What else did she teach you?* she wanted to ask, but then she reminded herself that she didn't really want to know. So many things we really don't want to think about in this world, she thought, such as our lover having had a lover before us; such as a mother quail bird returning to her emptied nest, peering under twigs and leaves and bits of grass for what she knew she had just left in there; such as the fact that every month Hillary carried fewer potentials inside of her ovaries; such as the fact that she sometimes felt panic over this, ever since nine months before when it just so happened that the important stuff had passed through Thomas to Hillary, but then the decision was made to end it there.

Thomas laughed at her now because her water was phlegmy and she hadn't even cooked her fish cakes. And by, *the decision was made,* she meant, *they had decided.* They were still new to each other back then; she wouldn't have dared pass gas in his presence yet. But now, to Hillary, that reason felt somewhat flimsy. Life should not be based on flatus or anything else that is passing and unseen, like fear, uncertainty. In these things is where all magic lives. Hillary waved away the Shabu waitress who held a pot of water above her bin.

"I want it phlegmy," Hillary said to her. The waitress looked confused. "I want it thick. I'm making myself a big, fat, ugly soup."

The waitress shrugged and walked away. Under his breath Thomas spewed a string of expletives and then laughed again.

Hillary knew he was referencing a joke she had once made some time before just after she had cooked for him some vichyssoise. "I make a mean soup," she had said; "it will tell you to fuck off if it gets truly angry."

She didn't laugh at this now and he asked her what was wrong.

"Nothing," she said, "I'm just sick of adding water. If I can't do it right I want to deal with it as is."

He told her that it was OK, because it was hard to get it right. He went on to say that Shabu was an art and not a science, and then he butchered Beckett's words about failure: *So you tried. So you failed. It doesn't matter. Fail better.*

"That's not how it goes," she said, which, he said, was his point exactly.

She wanted to tell him it had been nine months since that time they had decided. She wanted to tell him that her breasts swelled in false expectation just the other day, but at first she simply thought she had eaten too large an order of macaroni and cheese; but then later, when she lifted her cat and cradled him to her bosom for a moment, she imagined— and only for a moment did she imagine this—she imagined that he might suckle upon her. She quickly put him back on the floor. Dropped him, actually. He landed with a fat thud and shot her a dirty look.

This was not the sort of thing she would mention to Thomas, or anyone for that matter. For one, it was tremendously weird, and it made her feel like one of those people other people might avoid standing near to on the subway; and for two, he might feel badly about the whole goddamned incident and what good would that do now, to make someone she loved feel badly for an irreversible event? And for three, she was beginning to believe that we all experienced moments of confusion and inappropriate desire, and if we could hold these moments without hating ourselves, we'd come one step closer to beating that eternal loneliness of life.

This moment with her cat, disturbing as it might have been, was when it dawned on her—the forty weeks, the nine months. This was why she had once again become so fond of pineapple, grilled cheese. It was why she had eaten that entire plate of macaroni. This was why she kept crying on the phone to her sister every time that she called.

"Eat avocado," her sister told her. "It's good for anxiety."

"I have enough anxiety already, thank you," she replied, but she knew what she meant and started inhaling the fruit, or whatever the hell that pitted thing was. So much of life boils down to what we place in, and what we remove, from our anxious, bubbling, frightened cores. *Bumbling*, she meant, not *bubbling*. Hillary thought about this now as she ate her final slurp of vermicelli taken from the boiling pot before her.

Thomas said he was feeling full so he offered her his last quail egg. She took it in her fingers and he warned her to be careful because it might be hot, but it was only warm and she cupped it then inside her palms. She was always cold after Shabu-Shabu; leaning back from the steam always made her shiver, like she was placed down in the world just that very day, smack dab inside of winter, wearing only a spring jacket. She put the egg to the tip of her nose and rolled it down to her lips. Again he pulled her chair closer to his, and again he kissed her head. She slid the egg into her mouth and swallowed it along with all the stones that seemed to have gathered there—like a cairn, or some other rock pile that marked a grieving, or kept a tiny soul protected—inside her tightened throat.

dear england, please send me a redheaded boy

MUM

The way things are now I face Westville when I cook or when I soak my hands to wash a dish. Never heard of something quite so wrong, quite so dreadful—one should most certainly face *water* or *home*, and I should like to face home. Turn it, Old Man, and I will find you some help for the farm.

Dear England,

Please send me a redheaded boy, fire-red, please. We have one girl aflame but the others are stone yellow or dark as the sea. The flames are so easy to spot from afar.

We need help on the farm as our girls, strong they may be, are not quite of age to lift the hay that needs to be lifted. (The one with the man-hands is just a wee kid; give her a few seasons of sun and she'll hitch a small heifer on her back just to prove to her father that she can.)

Right now, I face Westville, but soon I'll face home, if you will only send a red boy to help the old man—that stick-of-a-man I see twigging by this west-facing window. We'll wait at the Cove for the boat to float into the embrace of our sweet treasure island. In my pockets will be food kept warm by my love.

JENNY

My Mum calls the new boy, Henry. His hair is like sticky candy and it is coarse when I run my fingers through the curls. He calls me Jenny-Man-Hands; I call him, Henry-Blood-Brother (B.B. for short), because we pricked fingers and touched the red drops, hot to hot, the very day he came. He's almost a man and I'm only nine. Right now I'm his sister, but I plan to be *wife* (don't mention this to him; he thinks I'm only a child).

I taught him to milk—pull the teats of the cow as if she has what he wants and he's taking it back. He won't speak of a mother other than mine. He won't tell of his father because now he loves mine, but he does talk of England, and how something so large can shrink to the glimmer of a small lighthouse flame when a boat pulls away—leaving outstretched arms of water holding on for dear life. Henry-Blood-Brother is now and forever; he is my candle, my love, my sweet brother on fire.

OLD MAN

The seas are threatening to drown the land; the land is warning of quakes and of cracking like eggs only thicker—rock off a cliff—and they call it *World War,* but my wife calls it *Timely,* says the church had predicted we'd go about now. I say that the cows are not showing a bit of fear and the cows always know—they will shake all of my milk into butter inside them if they sense a mighty storm, or a world-ending war.

I say the New Scots will be surely left standing as there is something special to the ways of our land, to the up and around green velvety hills and the drop-off cliffs where we kill all our sorrows. Furthermore, I am only a very old stick-of-a-man who cannot be bothered with war or of anything outside of here and of Westville where they all buy my milk for the good look of my cows. I'm also too busy to think of such things as Henry is talking of fighting for England and I must turn this house before he sets sail or I'll never quit hearing of facing old Westville when Mum cooks my food or washes my dish. She's a woman of principle, and despite all her moaning the one I will do most anything for.

HENRY

I have never let go of that English light. I have dreamt, every night, of those arms of water still holding the shoreline—wet fingers clutching with all of their might. I will fight just to see the land I adore. I will swiftly return, though, to this New Scottish cove, where my new father sells milk, my new mother warms food, and my sister will grow until she can lift a small heifer above her brown-as-oak head.

If the seas choose to flood and the land starts to quake, I will think of the gloaming that covers these cliffs where true sorrows are killed. This is how I first saw this land—the waves like great fists, foaming into the rock standing tall, holding Jenny-Man-Hands high on its shoulders. Such a wee kid; she was thrilled to have a brother at last. Should anything happen, should I be taken to the next world, I will leave word that my cap with the pins stuck to it should be sent back to Jenny, with all of my love.

HOUSE

They turned me the morning of no shadows—a few days before his soldier's death. My kitchen now faces the mother's home. *My* home is Westville, where I grew to be a grand old tree, where my roots continue to cling like hands to the wormy soil, where it is warm again, moist, and safe as a cave.

As slats, I am weak; damp air makes me warp. The jostle moved my joist span; the crane cracked my beams. This new gust of wind threatens my girders. I am as ill as the mother, who, because of my weakness, has caught the pneumonia and is waiting to die.

I can only allow her to peer from her death-bed through my square bedroom windows, and think of the bright flame-of-a-boy who became a mere flicker on the seas, and was snuffed out in England—a red puff of smoke that floated back up, as up is the only direction smoke knows.

the only lovely things about them

Margaret's arm brushed against Daniel's arm. She sat too near to him on the bench but if she shifted her body away from his body, she'd then be too near to Rooster, the left-handed woman who chose to sit on the far right because it was closer to the window. Each of them—Daniel, Rooster, and Margaret—held one hand out in front of them, palm side up, to cup a pile of silver straight pins. A taut sheet of plastic mesh, pulled flat by a frame, stretched before them, and into every other hole the three "Pinners" stuck an individual pin. The bed of pins they were making was nearly half-way finished and already Margaret thought the sculpture was a bit of a one-liner. But still, she enjoyed the rhythm of it all—one pin, two pin, *tap tap tap.*

The artist who designed the bed lived worlds away from the production studio and Margaret resented the fact that the woman's name would be on this piece which she would never assist in constructing; although, she thought, perhaps when it was finished the artist would run her soft flat hand across the million pins and catch a bit of skin and in this gesture, she would own it. Perhaps she'd look at this finished piece and see how much less fantastic it is in reality than it was in her head and feel that twist of disappointment one often feels when something dreamt is finally realized; and then, Margaret thought, she wouldn't simply *own* it, she'd be *responsible* for it. But what that meant, exactly, to be responsible for something, Margaret wasn't quite certain of.

Daniel sent a quick snort through his nose and looked up, away from the bed and toward the silk-screening tables by the far wall. Margaret knew he wanted her to prompt him to speak. She had been at this job for a week now and so she knew his ways.

"What is it, Daniel?" she asked.

"I was just thinking," he said, somberly.

"What were you thinking, Daniel?" She imagined the sound her rolling eyes would make if they actually made a sound—like a foosball dropping into a goal, a cold egg rocking in the bottom of a metal bowl.

"We could sue The Fabric Workspace because we're not even making minimum wage."

He spoke so slowly and mumbley it made Margaret's teeth clench.

"Yet it's under the table," she said, "and if you factor in the taxes it's kind of like minimum."

"Is it," he asked, as if it was a statement. "I don't know. Who has a calculator?" He turned his face to look at Margaret and she wanted to tell him to sit up straight; he looked like a tragedy. He was from Newfoundland, though, and on a high dosage of Prozac, so she let him slump.

Margaret sat up extra straight then and even leaned back a bit to allow Daniel to calculate the wages with Rooster, who claimed to be good at math. Rooster's real name was Rue, but on the first day of this job she had told the other "Pinners" that she always went by Rooster. She also said that she had just recently returned to Philadelphia from Israel where she volunteered to place gas masks on the faces of the insane in the case of a chemical bomb attack. She said the entire country had held its breath when the US attacked Iraq. Who knew what would happen? Margaret had to feign a cough to hide a laugh at the time that Rooster told her this, because she found herself imagining the girl sitting next to a mental basket case, holding two gas masks on her lap. It was, to her, a very funny scene. If she was a painter, she thought it would be the sort of thing she would paint; of course the basket case would be her mother, and Rooster would be an actual, true-to-life bird. She would title the painting, "The Volunteer."

Clink! Rooster dumped her handful of pins back into the can so that she could better calculate using her fingers and this irked Margaret to no end, as she believed that once the pins were in the hand they should continue this forward progression until they were into the mesh. The other "Pinners" had not found her same, efficient rhythm and the pin lines on the mesh were all wonky and uneven, like waves on a beach.

"It doesn't matter *any*way," Margaret said, a bit louder than she had intended. "Anyone who is here for the money is in*sane*." Rooster looked at her and so she said, "Not *clinically*, just, you know, not thinking clearly. This is a job you take to make your creative resume look interesting, or to get you out of the house until you decide what the hell to do with your life." She pulled a pin from in between her pointer finger and her curse finger and she tapped it into the mesh. She took another and tapped it, then tap tap tapped away.

"You're so much faster than me," Daniel said. She had nearly ten rows on him. He moved like a cat creeping to avoid an attack. If they were drinking and she was feeling fearless and a little mean, she'd tell him to seriously reconsider his dosage of antidepressant, but instead she showed him how, by lining the pins between her fingers like little warriors—the sharp points down, the flattened heads like silver caps—she could get a real system going which allowed her to zone out and move quickly. He acknowledged that it obviously worked for her, but then he continued to riskily pinch at the pile of pins—sticking every which way—cupped in the tender palm of his hand.

Margaret returned to her mother's home after her shift. She didn't mind returning to that home—she loved the broken tiles in the foyer and the sound of the wooden floor boards creaking beneath her weight—but she tensed for a moment as she waited for her mother to answer her "Hello."

"Hi," her mother hollered. Her voice sounded hot and echoic, but not overly forlorn, so Margaret thought: *In the tub.* "I'm in the tub," her mother said. "How was work?"

"Work," Margaret called up the stairs. "We're about half-way."

"And then what?"

"And then something else." She walked toward the kitchen and yelled, "Tea?"

"I'm drinking wine," her mother said. "I'm disgusting, I know. It's not even four o'clock."

"You're not disgusting," Margaret said. "It's exactly four." In the kitchen she poured a glass of wine for herself, too. It was the summer, after all. She had just graduated from college and her mother's husband had recently moved out. What the hell else was expected of her? Her fingers felt full of pins and she wondered if Daniel and Rooster felt pins in their own. She thought again of a painting she'd make if she were a painter. It wasn't as clear as the last one she had imagined, but it would involve people sitting in chairs, with their oversized hands resting upright in their laps. She'd call this one, "Four PM," or maybe just, "Hands."

Her mother joined her at the kitchen table shortly thereafter. She wore soft pants and slippers and Margaret thought that if she reached out and touched her that her skin would still be warm from the tub. Her mother took very hot baths. Margaret sometimes wondered if she took these hot baths when she had been pregnant with her. She wondered if that had anything to do with the fact that she had inherited none of her mother's creative talents—not one. While her mother could make anything—from gourmet food to heavy-lined curtains to puppets to carved stone sculptures—Margaret could only *imagine* the making. She failed miserably at the actual production of the creative thought, as if a talent got lost in her somewhere, as if it was burned right out of her very skin.

"You're not listening to me," her mother said. "You have become quite good at shutting me out."

She hadn't been listening and there was no sense in denying it, so she apologized and asked her to repeat what she had said.

"I was just saying that I remember now what book it was he had in his hand when he kissed me goodbye a week before he left. I saw the book in my mind but I couldn't for the life of me remember what it was. Well, now I remember." She stood and walked into the living room. She returned with a small, spiral-bound book, which she placed on the table in front of her daughter.

"Japanese Graveyards," Margaret read. "A Comprehensive Guide."

"Isn't that a kick in teeth?" her mother said. "It's like premeditated murder, only he didn't kill me, he left me." She sighed. "Not that I know for sure but jesus, it feels the same."

Margaret flipped through the book and mentally rolled her eyes at her mother's tendency to hyperbolize. The images in the book were breathtaking—reds and greens and browns so deep they looked unreal. She stopped on one image of a stone carving of a small animal—it looked like a dog, or a fox—that wore around its neck a lovely red bib.

"I guess he grew bored of my New Scottish ancestry and wanted to explore," her mother said, as if she knew the statement was ridiculous but she felt compelled to say it. "Oh, forget it," she said. She reached for the bottle of wine and poured some into her glass. "Anyway," she said, as she poured some then into Margaret's, "that's the book he was holding when he kissed me goodbye."

The next day Rooster called out sick so Margaret was able to scoot down further on the bench, closer to the windows and away from Daniel. At one point he asked her why she moved back home after graduation. He had stopped pinning and turned his head to look at her, his hand held out, full of pins, like he was offering them up to God himself.

"You can talk and pin at the same time," she said. "There is no need to look at me."

"I like looking at you," he said, although he turned his head back to the bed. "Besides," he said, "I have no interest in all these pins going into all these holes—I need a job and they're giving me no speed incentive."

"The only sort of speed incentive I imagine might work on you is if they had someone literally hold a flame to your ass." She laughed, but he didn't so she felt miserable for saying it. "Sorry," she said, "mean joke at your expense."

"Sorry," he said, "dumb joke regardless. So why'd you move home?"

"Why wouldn't I move home?" she said. "I can live for free." This was a lie, of course, because her mother couldn't manage the mortgage alone without her husband, and the small sum Margaret received at the Workspace all went toward that. "It's not about money, though," she said. "It's too sunny in California. There are too many goddamn chipper people zipping around."

"Oh, yeah," Daniel said, "that's exactly why I left New-foundland. Too many goddamn chipper people."

"Really?" she said, but then retracted it when she realized he was being sarcastic. She hadn't realized Daniel knew how to do such a thing. She knew, though, about Newfoundland from her grandmother—about the lack of fish and the overabundance of fishermen; about the high rate of alcoholism; about the excessive existence of Protestantism. It was the stuff of dreariness; this she knew.

"My grandmother was from Nova Scotia," she said. "We call it 'New Scotland.' Anyway, she told me Newfoundland was kind of down and out."

"That's cute that you call it New Scotland," Daniel said, a touch too mordantly for Margaret's taste. And then he added, "My father died by jumping off a cliff. Maybe he was trying to swim to your Grandma's blessed stomping grounds. You think that's a possibility?"

Margaret reddened. "No," and then, "I didn't mean to be flippant," she said. "Is that true? I'm so sorry. God." She turned and looked at him and considered telling him that she moved home because her mother's husband had called her the day before graduation to say that the cops had picked her mother up and were taking her to the hospital. Her mother had been walking down the street, half-dressed, drunk, holding a butter knife; she mildly threatened a group of Asian women who stood on the corner, waiting for the bus, and they had called the cops. Margaret didn't tell Daniel this, though, and instead just told him her mother lost her job when her husband left her. "She had worked for him," she said. "She helped to fabricate his sculptures in a foundry."

"What's she going to do now?" Daniel asked.

"He's a sculptor," she said.

"I got that," Daniel said. "You made that pretty clear."

What she meant to say was that she had loved his sculptures. What she meant to say was that she still did, even though he did leave her mother for a beautiful, young Japanese printmaker he met at the University at which he taught. What she meant to say was that this caused conflict within her—great storms of love and hate, admiring and despising, gratefulness and loathing. "She doesn't know what she'll do," she said. "She thinks perhaps the art world is corrupt and she should look into something different."

"Like what?" Daniel said.

"Like I don't know," she said. "Like I don't have all the answers for everyone all the time. Like that, ok?"

Daniel stuck a pin into the mesh and said, "Why are you working here?"

"I need art in my life," she said, knowing it sounded lame. Daniel snort-laughed, stuck a pin in a mesh hole.

When she got home that afternoon, Margaret moved directly toward the basement.

"What are you doing?" her mother yelled from upstairs. Her voice was low and cottony and Margaret thought: *In Bed.* "I'm in bed," her mother said.

"Laundry," Margaret yelled. She didn't walk toward the laundry, however; she walked toward the front of the house, where her mother's lovely pieces sat, dusted and unloved.

"Don't call them *pieces*," her mother once told her. "Art is not *pieces*. Brahms didn't compose pieces; Michelangelo didn't carve pieces. They made art. If you need to be specific be specific—sculpture, painting, song."

At the time, Margaret thought her mother was growing a god-like view of herself, a new-found sculptor, with a talent recognized by all who saw what she was beginning to make; but now, Margaret realized that she had simply been learning, coming to a new level of thinking about the created world. Her mother was a student, and this is what students do: they learn, they more *deeply* learn, and then they teach. Looking at what her mother had been making—what she had now ceased to make—made her feel deeply saddened, more so than she had expected when she started down the basement stair. They were strange little pieces, these things created by her mother—tiny effigies, distorted clay beings packed gently now in straw-filled boxes.

She turned, then, and moved toward a small alcove that at one time might have held wood for a fireplace. Now it held old beach chairs and board games. It also held—and Margaret knew this because she had placed it there—a large woodprint, left for her by her mother's husband. She pulled the print out from the cardboard sheets in which it was protected, and took it over to the laundry table. Even in the dim basement lighting she could see the brilliant colors and the variations in the texture of the ink—the mark of the pressure placed upon the wood by the press, by the artist. She ran her hand over the large, geometric blocks of green and red. She couldn't make it out before, but now she saw: A seated fox, wearing around its neck a lovely little red bib.

Rooster was still out the next day.

"Where is she?" Margaret asked Daniel.

"She left," he said. "She went back to the crazies in Israel."

"Jesus, why?" She sat down in the middle of the bench, not far away in Rooster's old seat.

"So she'd be closer to where she'll be of assistance when something catastrophic happens."

"*If* something catastrophic happens," she corrected. Her hands rested in her lap, pin-less and unmoving.

"She said when," Daniel said.

"Jesus," she said, "everyone's nuts."

"Are you asking or telling?"

"Shut up, Daniel."

He smiled and placed a few pins in the mesh. "I like how you say that," he said. "I like how you say my name."

"I say it like anyone would say it," she said.

"No," he said. "You say it sparingly, like it's precious or something."

"It's not *p*recious," she said, emphasizing her disgust with the p. "Daniel, Daniel, Daniel, Daniel…"

"Margaret, Margaret, Margaret," he said. The sound of her name made her throat ache, her eyes fill with tears. "I'll stop there," he said, and then they turned away from each other and they pinned.

Her mother sat in the living room, lacing her boots, when Margaret returned. Her mother smiled and said, "Oh there you are."

"Here I am."

"How was work?"

"Work," Margaret said. "There are only two of us now. That woman Rooster went back to Israel."

"Oh?" her mother said. "And what does that mean, then?"

Margaret hesitated. She noticed her woodprint, the fox with the bib, on the table beside her mother; she must have left it out the day before. "It means we have more room, I guess, for our elbows and stuff. Is that my woodprint?"

"No," her mother said. "It's *his* woodprint. The evil one whose name we shall not speak."

Margaret sensed a glass of wine or two in the statement. "I know it's *his*," she said, "but it's mine. I mean he left it for me."

Her mother looked perplexed and pre-hurt. "Well, yes, he left it, but I don't think he quite left it for you," she said.

"But it was in my room," Margaret said. "When I came home from school I found it in my room."

"But Maggie, it wasn't your room when you were away. I mean, it was when you'd come for a visit, but we often used it for storage. And for guests." She shook her head and scrunched her eyebrows down so that Margaret wasn't certain if she was angry or near tears. These days she floated from one to the other like a dingy boat in a storm. "I feel terrible that you thought he left this for you, Maggie. I really do. But believe me, he was not that caring of a man. Don't let yourself be fooled. Allow me to be the fool for the both of us."

Margaret sat in a rocking chair across from her mother and looked at the print. Then she noticed old tennis shoes, a dying plant, and a few books lay on the floor beside the table.

"Would you like to come with me?" her mother asked. She wore a smile that said, *please?*, and her hair curled out on one side more than the other. Her shirt collar, too, was askew. She laced her fingers on her lap and Margaret thought the existence of those fingers just might be the only lovely thing about her.

They came to the thrift store and Margaret thought: At least it's not a Salvation Army, or one of those crap holes on Girard that smell, quite literally, like ass. She thought this, yet still she felt uneasy about it. The shoes, yes—no one would want them anyway. The button-down shirts and faded leather belt, sure—perhaps someone could wear them to work. The dying plant, fine—although she wished they had simply put the plant out of its misery and donated the pot. But the print, no. It didn't feel right to donate the print. It didn't feel right at all.

"Margaret," her mother said. "The place is called Thrift Store For Aids. It's a positive move to donate here. Money from this piece will go to people suffering from Aids, and if art can help those people—"

"Don't say *piece*," Margaret mumbled.

"What?"

"You told me once not to say *piece*. It's a print; call it a print."

"Fine," her mother said. "Print." She turned to walk toward the donation drop-off desk and Margaret heard her add, "…Made by the devil incarnate whose name we shall not speak."

Margaret returned the next day, before her shift at the Workspace. Her eyes went immediately to the print, which stood propped on the top of a shelf that held old jelly jars and orange ceramics from the fifties. It looked like someone had connected the paper to a board with Bull-dog clips to hold it upright. Why didn't they simply poke a bunch of dull thumbtacks through it, Margaret thought, or smack it up on the wall with a wad of packing tape? The night before, when Margaret told her mother she thought they should return and get the print, her mother started to cry and said that she could have been one of those scorned women who just went and burned the man's things and that she thought she was being sane and reasonable by gently getting the hurtful things out of her house. Margaret thought that burning the print might have been more respectful, somehow, a ceremony of sorts. A definitive ending, a bit of ash and rising smoke.

"It'll help the *Aids people*, Margaret. I think it's a goddamn lovely gesture!" And then she cried harder and Margaret knew it was time to drop the subject altogether.

But standing there, now, looking at the print in the thrift store, her guts hurt too much to drop the subject—they hurt not for the artist, not for her mother, and not for herself—but for the print, for the intention behind the print, the intention for *art*. Whatever that word meant, whatever the importance of it, the intention to create it was there. She also, more immediately perhaps, hurt for the little blue/green fox on the paper, bowing his head toward a rusted silver pop-up toaster, and donning that ridiculous red bib.

"I have a favor to ask you."

Daniel lay face down on the bench, napping before his shift began. He didn't open his eyes when Margaret spoke, but lifted his arm and waved his hand to gesture for her to continue.

"It's more of a tip than a favor," she said. "A hot tip."

Daniel snort-laughed and unhurriedly opened his eyes

and rolled his face to look at her. "I'd rather the favor," he said. "I need no tips, but I don't mind doing a favor for you."

"I'm just saying that you'll get something out of it," she said.

He yawned, and in the tail end of the yawn said, "I know I'll get something out of it. I'll be doing something to help you. I'll be getting *that* out of it."

"What's that?"

"Satisfaction," he said.

"Stop being rural," she said. "Scoot over and let me sit."

Daniel laughed and sat up. "Rural? Is that like clueless or something?"

"No," she said, sitting next to him and brushing his hand away from where she wanted to put her legs. "It's like socially-awkward, or gullible or something, like you've spent too much time in the woods," she said. "Forget it. I shouldn't have said it. I heard some kid say it on the bus and I thought of you and so I said it. *Listen,*" she implored.

"OK, OK," he said. "The favor. Shoot."

First thing Margaret did was to describe his apartment, which she had never seen. She knew it was near her mother's home, in the Fairview section by the museum, but that it was in the section that had, at one point probably in the seventies, experienced some weird development experimentations that produced houses like those found in Manayunk and Roxborough—places where people covered porches with Astroturf and stuck plastic flowers into dirt-filled barrels.

"What I'm saying is: I suspect your apartment has white, textured walls and a thick gray carpet and windows with a thin dully-painted trim. If you have a sofa, it's probably off-white or tan and there's a crummy little island separating your kitchen from this monochromatic living room. Am I right?"

He paused, furrowed his brow. "Are these bad things?" he said. "Because having you say it like that makes me think that maybe they are."

"No, no, they're not bad, just a bit bland. Let me get to the point: You need some color on your walls."

"Hm," he said. "I have a Frantics poster on my walls. There's some red in it."

"A who?" she asked. She saw the man who hired them look at them and so she nudged Daniel and started pinning. "What's a Frantics?"

"A rock band," he said. "They're Canadian. Kind of like Rush, only better because they're Canadian."

"Oh, no," she said. "No. You are going to take that down and you are going to put something much better in its place. Much better. Art. Real art. You have to see it. It's at this thrift store for dirt cheap but I know the scoop on it."

He shrugged and placed a few pins into the mesh. He tapped them down dramatically. "I don't know," he said.

She looked at his fingers, lifting and tapping so extremely. They were knobby at the knuckles, confident and lean. This surprised her. "You'll have to see it," she said, unenthused, thinking this might not work.

"Only if you'll come with me," he said. "To see it."

She nodded.

"I was kidding," he said, softly. "About the poster. Yeah, I made it up. I don't have a Frantics poster up on the wall so let's go see this thing."

She turned her head to look at him. He was focusing on his pinning, but he smiled a bit and she thought he moved a little quicker than before. "Something different about you," she said. "What's different?"

He shrugged and told her to get to her pinning. She did, for a bit, but then she looked up and said, "Wow."

"What?"

"It's almost finished. The bed—it's almost all full of pins."

That night her mother came into her room at around three a.m. She sat at the foot of Margaret's bed and pulled her knees up to her chest. A sliver of light from a street lamp shone into the room and glinted off her face, which was soaked in tears or sweat or both. Margaret thought: *The three a.m. crazies.*

"I just keep going through those final weeks in my head, Maggie. I just keep figuring it out in hindsight, and in hindsight it's so glaringly obvious that he was going to leave I wonder if I'm all there up here."

She jammed her pointer finger to her head almost violently and Margaret thought, No, you're not. She sat up then and got a better look at her mother and noticed that her dampness was indeed from a mixture of sweat and tears.

"It's not hot, Mom. Why are you sweating?"

"I don't know," she said, dropping her head into her knees. "It comes over me like waves of hot water. Maybe I'm dying. Maybe he poisoned me and I'm dying."

"He didn't poison you, Mom. Stop exaggerating."

"Exaggerating? How am I exaggerating? He might as well have poisoned me—he took my life away! He took my job; he took my social circle. I'll probably lose the house. I feel crazy. I just feel completely like a crazy, sweaty, middle aged woman!"

She leaned a bit toward the head of the bed and Margaret scooted away from her. She thought if she reached out and touched her mother's skin that it would be hot. She didn't do this, however; instead she said, "Go back to your room, Mom. I need to work in the morning. "

Her mother looked at her, her eyes pained.

"Please," Margaret said. "Go."

She pinned slowly the next day, as did Daniel, although for him it was no different than before. The bed was nearly completed, with just a few rows of unpinned mesh remaining. Soon the tiny heads would be tarred over, the secured mesh flipped like a comforter and placed atop the bed frame. Soon it would no longer be a concern for Margaret—the pins, the strict adherence to one pin in every other hole, for even one misplaced pin in a million would interrupt the consistency of the illusion of softness. One misplaced point would shout to the observer: *sharp*, and *flawed*, and *made*.

After their shift, as Daniel puttered his Le Car down toward South Philadelphia, Margaret sat beside him thinking about her next job. Perhaps she'd go back to the Art School job board, where she found out about the position at the Workspace, and see if there is anything paint related that she could do. Maybe she was wrong; maybe she *could* paint under the right circumstances. Perhaps she could paint theatrically; perhaps her talents were hidden and simply needed some training. She thought like an artist; that she was sure of. She turned and looked at Daniel. The slump in his shoulders might be charming if depicted in the right manner, she thought, and who but an artist would think something like that? If she were to paint him she'd place him, standing, in a room full of balloons, or pillows— something soft and without sharp contour—so that his jaw and his shoulders, in comparison, might convey some resoluteness, strength. She'd call the painting, "Canadian Daniel."

"Why are you looking at me?" Daniel asked.

"I'm not," she said. "I was just thinking. What are you going to do next, I mean for a job?"

Someone in a Volvo cut him off and he had to slam on the breaks. Margaret held onto the door handle and marveled by how speedily he moved. He then honked the horn so limply, though, that it sounded long and wail-y, like someone blowing a large, cavernous nose.

"Take that," she mumbled, and then she laughed.

"My next job," he said, "will take me out to sea, where I will fish for shrimp on a boat named 'Moratorium.'"

She looked long at him and finally said, "In Newfoundland?"

He nodded.

Then she added, looking down at her hands, "With your father?"

He nodded again, but then he looked at her.

"Don't look at me," she said. "Drive your car."

"I like looking at you," he said, but then he took his eyes back to the road. "He *did* jump off a cliff," he said. "He just didn't die. Not physically, that is."

Margaret felt like she understood and didn't need to hear anymore. Her grandmother had told her about the suspension of cod fishing in the province. She told her how so many of the fishermen grew forlorn and defeated, and it made perfect sense to her that Daniel was a product of someone with this disposition.

"Nothing was done to them that they weren't participants in," she said now, thinking it might make him angry, and she wanted to make him angry because he had lied to her. "They over-fished and ignored the warnings, simple as that." And then she thought of her mother, felt angry that she had been so clueless when her own husband began to thin-out and fade-away. One should be able to read signs of impending disaster so one can either avoid it or run toward it, if running toward it is the more respectable option.

"You're right," Daniel agreed, "but my father was not strong enough to admit that he played a part in everything, at least not to others."

"Don't you think it's in bad taste to name the boat what he did?"

"Yes," he said. "But the other fishermen enjoy it and it creates a feeling of solidarity among them, I think. All I know is that he's no longer a zombie so I'm questioning nothing and going home."

"When are you leaving?" she asked.

"Soon."

"How soon?" But he just shrugged, turned and put his arm around her seat to back into a spot so tight, only a Le Car could fit.

Inside the thrift store, they found the print was gone. She looked at the spot in which it hung for a few days; in its place was a latch hook rug of a large yellow owl standing next to a smaller red one. The background was rust color and by the head of the large owl appeared a bright blue circle, which Margaret thought might be the moon. Daniel stood and looked for a moment and then walked toward the counter. As Margaret walked around the store, checking to see if perhaps the print had simply been moved, but knowing well that it hadn't, knowing well that someone—a student or a colleague of her mother's husband—had seen the print, seen his name on the print, and either purchased it or told him to come and purchase it. Again, she hurt, but this time it wasn't for the print or for the intention behind it, but for the artist himself, and for her mother, and a little bit for her.

Daniel walked up and placed his hand on her lower back. She turned and saw that he held the hook rug in his other arm. She began to tell him that that wasn't it—that wasn't the art she was bringing him to buy—but he shrugged and said that he liked it. He liked the blue circle and the smaller, red owl.

"I wonder who made it," he said. "Whoever made it did a really nice job. Really nice."

As they walked toward the car, Margaret told him that her mother had once taken her husband to Nova Scotia to show him the cemeteries in which her ancestors lay, and that they both came back with scarves made from the family tartan.

Daniel just looked at her and so she said, "I guess I told you that just to say that I think it's a nice idea that you're going home. Not that it matters what I think; I was just saying."

"Oh it does," he said. "It does matter what you think."

When they got to his home, she saw that his apartment was quite the opposite of what she had assumed—there were colors in everything: a red sofa, yellow chairs, a lavender afghan, a blue on blue checkered rug. He stood on an over-turned milk carton to hang the hook rug on the wall above his sofa. He stepped down and they looked at it; and when she saw how lovely it appeared on the wall—how fun and textured and hopeful, even—she came up behind him and wrapped her arms around his thin, hot frame. She moved her hands up under his tee shirt and felt his heart murmuring through his chest—she imagined she could feel his blood racing through his veins, his blood thick with drugs that made him slump but kept him away from something else, perhaps; something she felt drawn to but frightened of, as well. She moved to face him and his eyes were shut and damp in the corners. She kissed his jaw at the squarest point and she pulled him down with her to the blue, blue rug.

She reached down and undid his belt, his button-fly. He was soft in her hand, soft, even when she tried to take him fully inside of her. He whispered, shamefully, tried to explain about the drugs and their side effects, but she quieted him, kissed his mouth, and moved the softness out of him, unhurriedly, patiently, while saying in her head, over and over, for no reason that she could comprehend: *Newfoundland, Newfoundland, Newfoundland.*

When they got to their shift the next day they saw that the bed had been finished, a layer of tar spread drying over the heads. They had only left a row or two and they assumed that the production supervisors had been anxious to get to the next stage of fabrication so they could call the artist and tell her how close it was to *made.*

Daniel took a hold of her pinky finger and said, "I guess we're finished."

She nodded and said, "I guess we are."

He lifted her hand, placed the knuckle of her pinky in his mouth and rolled his tongue around it. She looked across the room at the other people working—students and graduates, interns and designers—all laboring on some aspect of some work of art for someone else: measuring cloth for silk screening; rinsing off printing blocks; untangling knots on a loom; stirring tar in a vat, growing high on the fumes. Sometimes our lives are so reliant on others, she thought; but then she wasn't sure if these folks were more reliant on the artists, or if the artists were more reliant on them. In either case, she felt ready to leave this place, as the air felt thick and hot.

As Daniel led her into the hall, toward the elevator, she thought of the artist of the pin bed coming to see it for the very first time. Would she feel a tinge of envy when she saw all those pins, thought of the many fingers behind them? Would she find fault with something in an attempt to participate? Or would she stand tall and proud, it being enough for her that when people spoke of her, they spoke of *the artist?*

Margaret hoped for the latter, because she felt it was true. She decided, then and there in the elevator descending, with Daniel's warm, lovely hand cupping her own, that if anyone asked her what earned someone the status of being an artist, if not the *making* of the art itself, she'd say the responsibility of *having* made, the burden of it—directly or indirectly, it didn't matter—for still there'd be this *made thing*, and there would be its makers, scrambling in their heads for the reasons why.

a note from the author

I would like to thank first and foremost, as a group, my original gangster family. I would also like to thank the lovely new gangsters who have become a sincere and important part of the crew. I thank my Big Mom-Mom Hill and Tony Petroski for both telling me that I should be a writer. I thank Uncle Jimmy for leaving all those crazy books around the house when he crashed with us. I thank my father for the flames in the fireplace and the chocolate sauce on the vanilla bean ice cream and oh so much more. I thank my sisters, Emily and Chrissy, for being so talented, supportive, beautiful, and just crazy enough to keep me going, and Emily for the amazing cover design. I thank Shawn Lyons for saving my butt and giving me work and being my friend when I needed it most. I thank Blair Waldmann for all the times he told me to take it easy. I thank Scott Ginder for saving that baby bird that flew into his apartment. I thank Terence Degnan for liking how I make up words. I thank Marcie Paper for reading so many of my words and looking so cute in dresses. I thank Amanda Tiller and Nicky Lorenzo for being such fabulously helpful tech geeks. I thank all of the members of The 6pm Sundays, Knitting Night, and The Rude Mares.

Pia Z. Erhrhardt, Kathy Fish, Anthony Tognazzini, and Alex Smith, I thank you for your time and your more-than-lovely words and your inspiration. Huge thanks to Kevin and the entire Press 53 Team! Your enthusiasm is astounding.

I thank the Michener Center for Writers, The Corporation of Yaddo, The Jentel Artist Residency, and VCCA.

And now, above it all, I thank the amazing woman who both made me and made me need and want to create: My beautiful, genius, introspective—*did I mention genius?*—mother, Elizabeth Jane Hill. What a wonder of a person you are.

KATE HILL CANTRILL lives in Brooklyn where she curates the Rabbit Tales Reading and Performance Series and is completing a novel. Her writing has appeared in literary publications including *Story Quarterly*, *Salt Hill*, *The Believer*, *Blackbird*, *QuickFiction*, *Mississippi Review*, *Smokelong Quarterly*, *Swink*, and others. She has been awarded fellowships from the Corporation of Yaddo, the Jentel Artists Residency, the Virginia Center for Creative Arts, and the James A. Michener Fund. She has taught fiction writing at The University of the Arts, The University of Texas, and the Sackett Street Workshop.

Cover Designer EMILY CANTRILL was born and raised in Philadelphia and has a strong background in the visual arts. She taught art for several years to elementary school students before studying at The Miami Ad School. She now works as a freelance designer. Her work appears regularly in both the Pennsylvania Ballet Playbill and the Pennsylvania Orchestra Playbill. She can be reached at cantrill.emily@gmail.com.